Willpower

An Original Play
about Marquette's Ossified Man

Written by Tyler R. Tichelaar

with Literary Passages by Will S. Adams

Directed by Moire Embley

Musical Direction by Jeff Bruning

Marquette Fiction
Marquette, Michigan

Willpower: An Original Play

For permission to perform *Willpower*, and all other inquiries, contact:

Tyler R. Tichelaar
Marquette Fiction
1202 Pine Street
Marquette, MI 49855
www.MarquetteFiction.com
tyler@marquettefiction.com

ISBN-13: 978-0-9962400-0-0
ISBN-10: 0-9962400-0-4

Library of Congress Control Number: 2015904936

Printed in the United States of America
Cover Image: Corey Sustarich
Interior Layout & Design: Larry Alexander
Publication managed by Superior Book Productions
www.SuperiorBookProductions.com

"Don't call me a cripple when you write your story, and don't say I am bedridden. I don't like those expressions. They put a fellow down too hard. And I'm not so badly off, you know. I'm not so badly off, old chap. Had it been otherwise, I might have become the subject of a trust investigation committee or a bank president. And I'd rather be literary than sordid any day."

— Will S. Adams, upon being interviewed by a reporter from the *Detroit Free Press* in 1906

Content

Note: The historic images on the lefthand pages before each scene are the photographic backdrops that were projected onto the stage during the performance. They are reproduced courtesy of the Marquette Regional History Center.

Production Notes

Willpower was first produced by the Marquette Regional History Center at Kaufman Auditorium in Marquette, Michigan, on September 18 & 19, 2014, with help from major grants from the Michigan Humanities Council, Upper Peninsula Health Plan, and Marquette County Community Foundation. Special thanks are also due to Forest Roberts Theatre, Westwood Shakespeare Company and B.G. Bradley, Marquette Senior High School, Lake Superior Youth Theatre, Messiah Lutheran Church, Bay Cliff Health Camp, Jim's Music, Marquette Arts & Culture Center, Togo's, Pride Printing, Corey Sustarich, Scott Taylor, and the J.M. Longyear Research Library.

The *Willpower* logo/front cover artwork was designed by Corey Sustarich. The sketched characters around the image were drawn by Will Adams and the photos are from the J.M. Longyear Research Library. They include Norma Ross, Sidney Adams, Harriet Adams, and Bertha Adams

Directors & Crew

Moire Embley	Director
Moire Embley	Technical Design
Jim Pennell	Sound & Light Design
Jeff Bruning	Original Composition & Musical Direction
Suzanne Shahbazi	Costume Design
Jalina Olgren	Stage Manager
Anna LaBreche	Assistant Stage Manager
Megan Hillier	Power Point Operator
Ben Hafer	Spot Operator
Kristen Ilves-Anderson	Hair Design
Shannon Jackson	Hair Design

Cast in Order of Appearance

Fred Rydholm	Dave Dagenais
Norma Ross (senior)	Jessica "Red" Bays
Grace Ross (senior & adult)	Monica Nordeen

Mather Hall Soloist..Patrick Leo Bradley

Will S. Adams (child)... Truman Durand

Norma Ross (child) .... Iris Oswald

Grace Ross (child) .... Senia Manson

Children's Choir..Tia Anderson, Ryleigh Jackson, Emma Bradley,
Gabrielle Langston, Elizabeth King, Truman Durand, Hunter Trepanier, Senia Manson, Jeremiah
Ogawa, Iris Oswald, Porter Bays, Emma Spade, & Ladyn Spade

Elsie ....Endla Harris

Minnie.. Tia Anderson

Nellie .... Ryleigh Jackson

Mary .... Emma Bradley

Ernie Ludlow (child) .... Jeremiah Ogawa

Joe .... Hunter Trepanier

Mrs. Ludlow & Harriet Adams ....Tiina Harris

Bertha Adams Beard ....Allison Hyttinen

Dr. James Dawson ....Anthony Pruett

Sidney Adams .... Chip Truscon

Will S. Adams (adult)... Andy Vanwelsenaers

Norma Ross (adult) ....Sara Parks

Dr. Eldred Robbins (Colonel Foster) ....Troy Graham

T.E. "Ernie" Ludlow (Lord Breakus) ....Anthony Pruett

Lillian Russell.. Isabel Francis

Telegram Delivery Boy .... Porter Bays

Rev. Bates Burt ....Martyn Martello

Understudies

Norma Ross (child) .... Ryleigh Jackson

Grace Ross (child) ....Tia Anderson

Will S. Adams (child)... Hunter Trepanier

Ernie Ludlow (child) ....Porter Bays

As depicted in *Willpower*, Norma Ross was presented with an award by Fred Rydholm, then mayor of Marquette, for her long service to the community in the form of the musical arts.

Later in the play, Norma shares information about the Adams family for Fred's book. Fred Rydholm would go on to become Marquette's most popular local historian. He would publish a two-volume history of Marquette County and the Huron Mountain Club, titled *Superior Heartland*, in 1989, which has gone through numerous printings. Fred passed away in 2009. He is shown here with the award he received from the Marquette County History Museum in 2009 "For Fostering Passion and Appreciation for Local History."

ACT I

Scene 1: Kaufman Auditorium, Marquette, Michigan, October 1963

[The curtain is down. Fred Rydholm, age thirty-nine and dressed as Mr. Lundie from *Brigadoon*, steps through the curtain with an award plaque in his hand.]

Fred: Welcome, ladies and gentleman. Tonight, we have a special treat for you. We are presenting the popular Broadway musical *Brigadoon*. As many of you know, I'm Fred Rydholm, and I will be playing the town of Brigadoon's local storyteller, Mr. Lundie, a role I'm told I'm well fitted for. But first, as Mayor of Marquette, it is my great honor to announce that this opening night performance is dedicated to someone very special to many of us in Marquette—Miss Norma Ross. Norma, I know you're out there in the audience somewhere. Would you come up on stage for a minute?

[Applause as Norma, in her eighties, comes up on stage, assisted by her sister Grace. Norma walks up to Fred and bows to the audience.]

Fred: In case there is anyone out there who doesn't know, Norma is retired from the Marquette Public Schools where she spent forty-four years as a music teacher, leading the school choirs, and starting the first orchestra. She's also been heavily involved in community music and theater productions and her church choir. And not only was she my music teacher in school, but she was my father's music teacher. And I bet most of you in this room tonight had her as your music teacher. It might not even be too much to say that we wouldn't be performing this wonderful production of *Brigadoon* tonight if it weren't for Norma's commitment to keeping music an integral part of this community. Therefore, the City Commission of Marquette has adopted a resolution to honor Miss Norma Ross for her...well, I better read it so I don't mess it up. [He lifts up the plaque to read it.] For her "unselfish and dedicated devotion to the children of our community in the training and development of their musical talent and music appreciation, thereby in part being responsible for the many excellent musical programs which the people in this area have enjoyed over a period of many years."

[Fred hands the award to Norma as the crowd applauds.]

Norma: Thank you, Fred, and I'm glad to see that despite all my efforts, the director, Mrs. Lasich, was smart enough not to give you a singing role in *Brigadoon*. [Laughter from everyone. Fred's laughter is the loudest.] What can I say except to thank you profusely and to tell you all that it has been my pleasure to be a part of this community and champion its music programs. Music has been what has kept me going all these years. The great blessing and privilege of my life has been the opportunity to pass it on to others. I also had one great inspiration. How I wish you were here with me tonight, Will

Adams. You helped so much to make music and literature and theatre a strong part of this community. I thank you all for both of us, and I hope music remains a part of this community long after I'm gone.

[Norma and Grace begin to walk back to their seats.]

Fred: Thank you, Norma. And now the Marquette Community Theatre is proud to present *Brigadoon*!

[Fred exits through the curtain.]

Grace: (turning to her sister) Norma, Father would be so proud of you. He helped bring music and theatre to Marquette, but you've helped keep it alive all these years.

Norma: Well, I had a lot of help. I remember first meeting Will at Father's theatre as if it were only yesterday.

Marquette's Graveraet School includes Kaufman Auditorium (right wing) and the Sidney Adams Gymnasium (left wing). Kaufman Auditorium was named for Louis Kaufman, brother to Mayor Nathan Kaufman, whom Will draws in the play. The auditorium is where Norma Ross received her award during the production of *Brigadoon*. It's also where *Willpower* premiered. According to Fred Rydholm in *Superior Heartland*, Harriet Adams donated the land for the gymnasium on the condition that it be named for her late husband.

Exterior of Mather Hall

Marquette Opera House interior used as Mather Hall interior in *Willpower*

Scene 2: Mather Hall, Mr. Ross's Theatre, 1892

[Will, age fourteen, has sneaked into the theatre. He is hiding backstage, watching a singer perform the end of "After the Ball."]

Singer:

> A little maiden climbed an old man's knee,
> Begged for a story—"Do, Uncle, please.
> Why are you single; why live alone?
> Have you no babies; have you no home?"
> "I had a sweetheart years, years ago;
> Where she is now pet, you will soon know.
> List to the story, I'll tell it all,
> I believed her faithless after the ball."
>
> After the ball is over,
> After the break of morn—
> After the dancers' leaving;
> After the stars are gone;
> Many a heart is aching,
> If you could read them all;
> Many the hopes that have vanished
> After the ball.

[As the song ends, Norma and Grace, her younger sister, approach Will.]

Norma: (tapping Will on the shoulder and whispering) You can't be back here.

[Will turns around, embarrassed, but trying to joke his way out of the situation. His manner is grandiose, confident, but not off-putting.]

Will: (speaking boldly rather than whispering) Ah, but you see, there's where you're wrong. You say I can't be back here, but I am here, so it is possible. I *can* be back here.

Norma: I mean, no audience members are allowed backstage.

Will: But how am I to become a famous playwright if I don't know what goes on backstage? I'm sure you wouldn't want to be remembered as the girl who thwarted a great playwright's future by tattling on me, now would you?

[Norma looks taken aback by his verbosity and confidence, but Grace is unimpressed.]

Grace: Did you sneak in? My father owns this theatre, and if you snuck in, you're going to be in trouble.

Will: But I've already seen the play from the seats, so I thought I'd get a different perspective of it from behind the scenes. To be a playwright, I need to know everything about a play and not just what the public sees.

Grace: You don't have permission to be back here.

Norma: (softer and feeling a bit dazzled) You want to be a playwright?

Will: I do, and don't you think it's fitting? After all, the great Bard of Stratford-on-Avon and I share the same name.

Grace: What? The bard of what?

Norma: Grace, I think he means Shakespeare. [She turns to Will.] So I guess that means your name is William?

Will: Just Will to my friends, and I can tell we are going to be fine friends when a lovely lady like yourself understands so well my frame of mind.

Norma: (suddenly realizing to whom she's speaking) Oh, I know who you are. You're Will Adams. I've heard you sing in the boys choir at St. Paul's. You have a beautiful voice.

Will: Thank you. But with all due respect to the Creator, I believe singing hymns limits me, which is why I secretly wish to write a musical comedy.

Norma: Oh, that's wonderful. I love musical theatre, especially operettas. They're very romantic.

Will: Then, my dear, just to please you, I shall make it an operetta. I will make it light and humorous and full of beautiful music that makes one's heart soar.

Grace: The play being performed right now is a musical comedy, but that song "After the Ball" isn't a happy one.

Will: It is bittersweet, yes, but it is has truth in it. People who chase after love are bound to have their hearts broken, yet I confess I am a romantic myself.

Norma: I think love is grand. And I've often thought that the need to express one's love is what first made people create music.

Will: Spoken like a poetess, my dear, although you are far too young to know anything about falling in love. [He bends and kisses her hand and she laughs.]

Grace: (shocked) I'm going to tell Father. He won't like that, Norma. You're too young to have a beau.

Norma: Hush, Grace. We're just playacting.

Will: I hope not. Acting is a serious business, and so is love, or so I've been told.

Grace: Shh, the next act is starting. [She peers through the curtain at the stage.]

Will: I'm afraid I must be going. I have to be home by dark, but I thank you for not tattling on me.

Norma: Oh, you have to stay for the next act. It's hilarious.

Will: I've already seen all the things I can love for one evening. Good night.

Norma: Wait. When will I see you again? I mean, maybe we could sing together some time. I also sing in my church choir.

Will: That, my dear, would be magnificent—to hear you sing, I mean. I will look forward to it and trust that the stars will cross properly so as to bring it about.

[As he starts to leave, Norma notices that he limps.]

Norma: Oh, did you hurt yourself?

Will: Just a little baseball injury. It's nothing. Should be all healed in a day or two. Good night.

Grace: (sourly) Good night.

Norma: Oh, Grace, isn't he nice? And he's both artistic and athletic.

Grace: (loudly) He's no account, Norma, if he sneaks into theatres.

Norma: Shh, the audience might hear you. Besides, he's the mayor's son, you know.

Grace: (rolling her eyes) Then he should know better.

Front Street

Scene 3: Downtown Marquette, 1892

[Grace and Norma are walking down the street. Norma is humming "After the Ball."]

Grace: Will you quit that? That show quit playing weeks ago, and I'm sick of hearing you humming that tune all the time.

Norma: I don't care. It's a beautiful song. If you don't like it, you have no taste in music.

Grace: It's not my taste in music that's the problem. It's your taste in boys. I know why you keep humming that song.

Norma: (looking astonished) What do you mean?

Grace: (accusingly) You know what I mean. I think you're sweet on someone.

[Will approaches on crutches.]

Norma: (to Grace, upon seeing Will) Shush.

[Grace, looking frustrated, is about to turn and go the other way, but it is too late because Will has seen them.]

Will: Why, hello there, Poetess. I told you the stars would align for us to meet again, and it's only been three weeks.

Grace: (sarcastically) I guess the stars are kind of slow.

Norma: (elbowing Grace) Will, did you hurt yourself again?

Will: Oh, it's nothing. The same little injury. The doctors don't know why my leg has stiffened up, but I'm going to shake it yet. [He laughs and shakes his head as if to demonstrate since he can't shake his leg.]

Norma: Does it hurt?

Will: Just physically. Actually, no. The funny thing is I can't feel anything in my leg. The doctor says it has positively ossified.

Norma: What does "os-si-fied" mean?

Will: Just that it's hardened and become brittle. But I'm not going to let it keep me from doing anything. I might not be able to dance, but I can still sing and draw cartoons and write stories.

Norma: Oh, you write stories? I thought you wanted to write plays.

Will: I don't see any reason to limit myself. I intend to create all kinds of literature, art, and music. A stiff leg won't stop me from penning the great American novel or the next winning operetta.

Norma: You have such big dreams.

Will: Well, what's the point of having a dream if it isn't big?

Norma: Oh, I like that you dream big.

Will: Good. If you really want to live, you have to dream big. Too many people walk around like they're carrying the weight of the world on their shoulders because they're afraid to dream. That's not the kind of life I want. I plan to do everything the Good Lord gives me time to do. How about you?

[Grace is tapping her foot, arms crossed, and looking impatient as Will gives the above speech.]

Norma: (looking confused) What do you mean?

Will: What are your dreams?

Norma: Oh, I don't know.

Will: Now, don't be shy. You haven't laughed about mine so I won't laugh at yours. Tell me.

Norma: Well, I—

Will: Come on. Say it straight out, loud and bold.

Norma: Okay, I will. (In a loud voice) I want to be...an opera singer.

Will: (trying to clap his hands so that he almost falls over as he lets go of his crutches) Splendid! Splendid!

Grace: You can't be an opera singer. Who ever heard of an opera singer coming from a little town like Marquette? You have to go to New York or Paris to be an opera singer.

[Norma's shoulders start to sag in defeat.]

Will: (to Grace) And who, little lady, says that your sister can't go to New York or Paris? Do you want to be the killer of your sister's dream?

Grace: Well, I'm just—

Will: I thought not. Now what are you doing, Norma, to make your dream come true?

Norma: (laughing) What are you doing to make yours come true?

Will: Why, all kinds of things. Sneaking into your father's theatre to watch plays for one, and I plan to start up a literary magazine someday, and in the meantime, I'm drawing cartoons for it, and learning everything about literature that I can.

Norma: Like what?

Will: Like reading Shakespeare and Dickens—but you still haven't told me what you are doing to make your dream come true, Norma.

Norma: Well, I sing in the church choir.

Will: Very good. What else?

Norma: Um...nothing else that I can think of.

Will: That's not true. You're having this conversation with me, and while you're having it, you're thinking about your dream and that's the surest way to make it happen. You just need to believe it will happen. Someday, I'm going to write an operetta and see you star in it. You just see if I don't.

Norma: (embarrassed by his attention) Are you still singing in the boys' choir too, Will?

Grace: Norma, let's go. We'll be late getting home and we have to help Mama peel the potatoes for supper.

Norma: Grace, don't be rude. It's not ladylike.

[Grace rolls her eyes and pouts.]

Will: Yes, yes, I am still singing. In fact, we're having a concert tomorrow night at St. Paul's. Why don't you come?

Grace: We're Baptists. We can't go to the Episcopal Church.

Will: Why ever not? God goes to both churches.

Norma: (laughing) He's right, Grace.

Will: Come tomorrow night at seven o'clock.

Norma: Okay. I will. And I'm singing at my church on Sunday if you would like to come.

Grace: I don't think they let Episcopalians into the Baptist Church.

Will: Then I shall convert just for this one Sunday.

Norma: Please do come, Will.

Will: It's settled then. I'll see you tomorrow night, and I'll sing directly at your pew. Until then....

Norma: Until then.

[Will makes his way off stage. Norma and Grace start to exit in the opposite direction.]

Grace: Norma, Father wouldn't like you having a beau.

Interior of St. Paul's

Will Adams in his St. Paul's boys choir robe

Scene 4: St. Paul's Episcopal Church, 1892

[A boys' choir is on one side of the stage and a girls' choir on the other. Norma and Will enter together from the side. Will is still using his crutches.]

Norma: I'm so excited that your church invited our choir to come sing with yours.

Will: Yes, and such a great song, too.

Norma: It's always been one of my favorites.

Will: And best of all, it captures my belief about life. No matter what goes wrong in life, there is so much to be happy and grateful for.

Norma: Even though your leg doesn't seem to be healing?

Will: (grimacing from dislike of being reminded of it) It doesn't hurt much. As long as I can sing, why let it fret me?

[As they speak, the choir director has come on stage. He now motions to them.]

Choir Director: Places, please.

[Will and Norma take their places in front of the respective boys' and girls' choirs and they all begin to sing.]

Will:

    My life flows on in endless song;
Above earth's lamentation.

Norma:

    I hear the real though far-off hymn
That hails a new creation.

Full Choir:

    No storm can shake my inmost calm,
While to that rock I'm clinging.
    Since Love is Lord of heaven and earth,
How can I keep from singing?

Through all the tumult and the strife,
I hear that music ringing;
It sounds and echoes in my soul;
How can I keep from singing?

No storm can shake my inmost calm,
While to that rock I'm clinging.
Since Love is Lord of heaven and earth,
How can I keep from singing?

What though the tempest 'round me roar,
I hear the truth it liveth.
What though the darkness 'round me close,
Songs in the night it giveth.

No storm can shake my inmost calm,
While to that rock I'm clinging.
Since Love is Lord of heaven and earth,
How can I keep from singing?

The First Baptist Church – circa 1900. This church stood on N. Front Street where the Landmark Inn's parking lot is today. Norma Ross was a lifetime member of the congregation, both at this church, which was built in 1886 and burned down in 1963, and the second church built on Kaye Avenue.

The Sidney Adams residence and St. Paul's Episcopal Church directly across the street. Rumor is that Mr. Adams had a tunnel built between the house and church so the family could take Will to church in the winter. (Photo Courtesy of Jack Deo)

Washington Street

Scene 5: Downtown Marquette, Valentine's Day, 1893

[Norma, Grace, and their friends Elsie, Minnie, Mary, and Nellie are out window shopping.]

Elsie: (gushing overdramatically) Don't you just love Valentine's Day? I think it's the most romantic thing ever invented!

Minnie: (rolling her eyes) Why? So you can have some runny-nosed boy give you a Valentine after he's wiped his nose on his hand? Gross.

Nellie: Oh, Minnie, you haven't a romantic bone in your body.

Minnie: Not after that nasty Joe wanted to give me a dead mouse for Valentine's Day last year.

Elsie: Well, I don't like dead mice myself, but it's the thought that counts.

Mary: Stop being silly, Elsie. My mother says we're much too young to be thinking about beaus.

Nellie: (looking down at her chest) Not me. I'm developing early, my mother says.

Minnie: Shh, don't talk like that. What if someone heard you?

Mary: Yes, Nellie. It's not ladylike and just shows your imma...immatcha... (trying to pronounce it).

Norma: Immaturity.

Mary: Yes, immaturity.

Elsie: You're awful quiet on the subject of Valentine's Day, Norma....

Grace: She better be. She wanted to send a Valentine's Day card to—

Norma: Grace, be quiet. That's no one's business but mine.

[As the girls argue, Will, in his wheelchair, approaches them.]

Elsie: Send a card to who?

Nellie: Yeah, Norma. Do you have a secret beau?

Grace: She wanted to send a card to—

Norma: (getting in her sister's face) Grace, I'm warning you.

Will: Norma!

Elsie: Who's that?

Grace: The boy she wanted to—

Norma: (turning and seeing Will and also purposely interrupting her sister) Will! Will, what are you doing out?

Will: What do you mean? You act like it's a bad day. It's a comfortable 27 degrees. Prime mid-February weather, and there's hardly a snowflake on the sidewalks.

Norma: But are you by yourself?

Will: Norma, I'm almost fifteen. I'm not likely to get lost downtown.

Norma: But how did you get here?

Will: Why, I wheeled myself here.

Norma: All the way from your house?

Will: Yes, I admit it got a bit hairy coming down the hill on Front Street—thought I might break my neck actually, but Mr. Kaufman got in my way and provided a good stopper for me, though perhaps not so good for him. I'm afraid he tore his trousers.

[The girls all start laughing except Norma, who shows concern.]

Norma: Girls, can't you see we're having a private conversation. Could you show some manners?

Elsie: Come on, girls. Norma wants to talk to her beau.

[The girls laugh and exit, leaving Norma blushing.]

Will: Well, I'm glad they're gone. I was hoping to catch you alone for a minute.

Norma: Will, why would you do such a dangerous thing—coming down Front Street in your wheelchair?

Will: (saying it like it's the most obvious thing in the world) Norma, it's Valentine's Day.

Norma: So?

Will: So, I saw you walk by the house and needed to catch you.

Norma: Why?

Will: To give you this. [He reaches into his coat and pulls out a Valentine.]

Norma: Oh, Will, no one ever gave me a real Valentine before.

[She looks at it lovingly as Ernie and Joe, boys about twelve to fourteen years in age, come down the street in their direction.]

Ernie: Joe, look at that. Norma's got a cripple for a boyfriend.

Norma: (turning on the boys) He is not a cripple. He had a baseball accident. He's going to get better.

Ernie: Baseball accident?

Joe: Yeah, he's Will Adams. He was one of the best ballplayers in Marquette until he became a cripple.

Norma: (adamantly) He's not a cripple.

Will: (grabbing her arm to calm her) It's okay, Norma.

Norma: It isn't okay. (speaking to Ernie and Joe directly) You can't just go around town calling people names like that.

Ernie: Don't get so worked up about it, Norma. I'm just telling it like it is. It's not like he can take you ice skating and spooning after dark like I can.

Norma: Spooning? What makes you think I'd want to go spooning with you?

Ernie: How do you know you don't want to until you try it? (He steps in and tries to put his arm around her waist.) We'll go ice skating until you're good and cold, and then my kisses will warm you right up.

Norma: (pulling away from him) You know something, Ernie Ludlow, you're—

Will: Norma, please.

[Norma closes her mouth.]

Ernie: I guess the cripple is your boyfriend if you're going to do what he tells you.

Norma: And what if he were my boyfriend, Ernie Ludlow? He's twice the man you are. He's strong and kind and brave, and he has a beautiful singing voice, and—

Ernie: Singing's for sissies.

Joe: Yeah, singing's for sissies.

Norma: (to Ernie) That's funny since I heard you humming the other day.

Ernie: Humming's not singing. And I can run and jump and that's more than he can.

Norma: Why don't you go jump off a cliff then!

Will: Come on, Norma. Let's go. [Will turns his wheelchair in the other direction to leave.]

Ernie: That's right, Sissy. Run away since your girlfriend can't protect you.

[A woman enters from the direction Joe and Ernie came.]

Woman: Ernest Ludlow, you get over here right this minute. Why, I've been looking all over for you for the last half hour. Just you wait until I tell your father how you took off on me. I hate to think what he's likely to do to you.

[Ernie, looking nervous, heads toward his mother as the girls return.]

Ernie: Mama, you don't have to tell Father, do you?

[Norma snorts with laughter, then shouts after him.]

Norma: Who's a sissy now?

Nellie: What's going on?

Mary: What was all the shouting about?

Norma: Never mind. It's none of your business.

Joe: (stepping up to Minnie) I was looking for you, Minnie.

Minnie: (angry) Why?

Joe: (digging in his coat pocket) I—I wanted to give you this.

Nellie: (laughing) What is it? Another dead mouse?

Joe: (pulls a crumpled Valentine from his pocket). No, this. I want to know if you'll be my girl.

[Minnie looks at the pathetic Valentine, rips it out of his hand, tears it in pieces, and tosses it back at him.]

Minnie: I wouldn't be your girl for ten thousand Valentines, Joseph Snot-Nose.

[Minnie stomps off. All the girls follow her except Elsie, who looks down at the Valentine sadly. Joe, crestfallen, begins to exit.]

Elsie: (running after him) Joe, wait! Do you want to come over to my house? My brother has a pet frog.

[Joe nods his head and Elsie takes his hand. They exit together.]

Will: Norma, you shouldn't have done that—told off Ernie that way.

Norma: Why not?

Will: What if he and Joe had hurt you? I'm not really in a position to protect you.

Norma: I'm not afraid of them. Bullies are just cowards.

Will: (with mock admiration) Well, now, I can see just how wise you are, and strong too, I daresay, for a girl.

Norma: Don't you start in on me too, Will.

Will: Start in on you, my best girl? Absolutely not. Why, you have the makings of an Amazon warrior. I suspect you're even strong enough to push me back up Front Street.

Norma: (assessing the situation) Oh, well, I'll give it a try.

[Norma steps behind the wheelchair and starts pushing Will offstage.]

Will: By the way, I was just joking about riding down Front Street in my wheelchair. Father pushed me down on his way back to the office after lunch.

[They exit.]

Sidney and Harriet Adams were true pioneers of Marquette. He arrived in Marquette in 1850 at age nineteen, and in 1857, he married and brought his wife to Marquette. He was involved in potato farming, mining, and timber, and he served as Marquette's mayor in 1896. Mr. Adams wasn't all business, however. His heart was big enough to adopt the orphaned Will, and he indulged in designing terraces on the hill behind his house, filling them with fruit and vegetables, as well as building bridges for people to walk on. He extended the terraces not only behind his property but behind many more houses extending eastward along Ridge Street. His son-in-law, Dr. Dawson, in a historical paper on Early Pioneers of Marquette, described him as "small in stature, never of constitution, of a nervous temperament, still always self controlled, with a winning smile."

Sidney Adams' terraced gardens (Photo courtesy of Jack Deo)

Adams House Exterior

Image used for Adams House interior, actually the historical Jaedecke Home at 223 Barnum in Ishpeming, MI

Scene 6: The Adams House, 1893

[Will is seated in a wheelchair, drawing with a pad on his lap, when his sister Bertha, who is twenty-seven, enters the room. She is wearing black to show she is in mourning for her late husband.]

Bertha: Will, Mother says the doctor will be here shortly.

Will: (preoccupied with his drawing) Oh, all right, Sister. Thank you.

Bertha: Will, what are you drawing?

Will: All of my acquaintances in Marquette. Don't you recognize them?

Will's drawing of Nathan Kaufman

Will's drawing of Peter White

Will: Do you see anyone you know?

Bertha: Why, Will, I believe that's Mr. Nathan Kaufman and Peter White.

Will: I see you have an observant eye, Bertha.

Bertha: But why are you drawing them, Will?

Will: Just for fun, and you know, so I don't forget their faces.

Bertha: Don't give up hope, Will. I pray every day that you'll walk again, and Father said we can get you a special bed so we can carry you to church and other places.

Will: I'll keep drawing anyway. You know I plan to launch a literary magazine and draw the cartoons myself.

Bertha: You sure are ambitious for such a young man.

Will: Ambitious and talented, I hope.

Bertha: Yes, talented. Will, do you think you could draw a portrait of George for me?

Will: (hesitating) Bertha, I think it's time you quit thinking about poor George and start thinking about finding a new husband.

Bertha: Oh, I couldn't, Will. It wouldn't be—

Will: (interrupting and speaking firmly) George wouldn't want to see you moping and alone, Bertha. It's been nearly three years now.

[Mrs. Harriet Adams enters.]

Mrs. Adams: Will, Dr. Dawson is here to see you. You know I thought we should get another opinion on your condition.

Will: All right, Mother, although I doubt Dr. Dawson will know any more than all the other doctors.

[Mr. Sidney Adams enters with Dr. Dawson, who is carrying his medical bag. Both have beards. Will has his drawings in his lap and sets them down on a chair or table nearby.]

Mr. Adams: Right this way, Doctor.

Dr. Dawson: (stepping up to Will to shake his hand) Hello, young man. I'm Dr. Dawson.

Will: Young man? You don't look all that old yourself. How old are you?

Dr. Dawson: Thirty. Almost thirty-one. And I've been practicing medicine for almost eight years.

Will: Well, I guess I won't hold your youth against you. After all, I'm only fifteen and already a literary genius.

Mrs. Adams: (disapprovingly) Will, be polite.

Will: Am I not a literary genius?

[Mrs. Adams gives Will a disapproving look.]

Mr. Adams: It's all right, Harriet. The boy won't get anywhere in life if he doesn't believe in himself.

Dr. Dawson: And just where do you want to get in life, Will?

Will: Well, Doctor, just getting out of this wheelchair would be great for starters.

Dr. Dawson: Yes, I imagine it would be, but from what I understand, your body is slowly ossifying; your legs have hardened to the point where it's unlikely you'll ever walk again, and over time, the ossification will probably work its way up the rest of your body.

Will: You sure don't beat around the bush, Doctor, despite that bush hanging from your face.

Dr. Dawson: There's always hope, Will, but there's also facts. I wouldn't give up hope, but you have to accept the situation until we can determine what is causing the ossification.

[Mrs. Adams starts to tear up.]

Will: Now, don't cry, Mother. That won't help anything. You have to keep your spirits up. I want smiles, not tears, and lots of laughter. No one ever got better by crying.

Dr. Dawson: I understand, Will, that you've been examined thoroughly by several prominent physicians who have all poked and prodded you, and they all say they can't explain the cause of your condition.

Mr. Adams: Actually, Doctor, one of the physicians thought it might be the result of a baseball injury Will had.

Dr. Dawson: (to Mr. and Mrs. Adams) It's possible, but can you tell me anything about your family's medical history? Is there any arthritis, rheumatism, paralysis of any sort in the family?

Mrs. Adams: I'm afraid, Doctor, that we adopted Will when he was a little boy. We don't know anything about his parents' medical history.

Dr. Dawson: I see.

Will: Now, Doctor, don't go thinking I've had it extra hard being adopted and ossified. Look at this beautiful house I get to live in, and from our porch, I can look down at that busy harbor, and my father knows all the great men in this town so I've had plenty of opportunities and made plenty of friends.

Dr. Dawson: And very good spirits too, I see.

Bertha: No one has a spirit like Will. I don't know how I'd have managed after my husband died if he hadn't always been cheering me up.

Dr. Dawson: (noticing for the first time that she is wearing black) I'm sorry to hear of your loss, Mrs....

Bertha: Mrs. Beard. Thank you. It's been nearly three years since I lost George, but Will has helped me and all of us to get through that and all our other difficulties.

Mr. Adams: He's a very clever boy, Doctor. We're all very proud of him.

Dr. Dawson: (smiling) Yes, I can imagine you are. Now, if you don't mind, ladies, I would like to examine Will in private.

Mrs. Adams: Certainly, Doctor.

[Mrs. Adams and Bertha withdraw. Mr. Adams helps Dr. Dawson lift Will from his wheelchair and places him on the sofa. Dr. Dawson takes his hammer from his bag to check Will's reflexes while Mr. Adams departs.]

Dr. Dawson: Tell me if you can feel anything, Will. Do you feel that? How about that?

Will: No, nothing, Doctor.

Dr. Dawson: No pain? Not even the slightest tingle?

Will: No, Doctor. Nothing.

Dr. Dawson: Tell me when you do feel something. How about here?

Will: No.

Dr. Dawson: Here?

Will: No.

Dr. Dawson: How about here?

Will: No. Nothing.

Dr. Dawson: And what about here?

Will: Yes, there doctor.

Dr. Dawson: Right by the thigh. Okay. Then we know how far the illness has progressed. Six months ago, your father said you could feel everything above your knee.

Will: (sounding grim) Yes, Doctor.

[Dr. Dawson sits beside Will on the couch and puts an arm around him.]

Dr. Dawson: Cheer up, Will. It's going to be okay.

Will: I don't mind the not walking part, Doctor, but it's embarrassing to have my family see me like this.

Dr. Dawson: I'd say you're very lucky, Will, to have a family who cares so much about you.

Will: I know. I love them all dearly. I wish my sister would get married again, though. She shouldn't mourn like she does.

Dr. Dawson: She appears to be still very young.

Will: Three years younger than you, Doctor.

[Mr. Adams enters the room.]

Mr. Adams: (quietly but looking hopeful) Well, Doctor?

Dr. Dawson: (shaking his head sadly) Mr. Adams, it's times like these when I wish I had chosen a different profession. I've heard of similar cases, but no one understands the cause nor knows the remedy for this ailment.

Mr. Adams: (hanging his head) That's what all the doctors have said, but I appreciate your time.

[Bertha enters the room with a tea tray.]

Bertha: Dr. Dawson, won't you stay for tea?

Dr. Dawson: Thank you, Mrs. Beard, but I'm afraid I have other patients to see.

Bertha: Some other time then? [She crosses to him and takes his hand in her own.] I do hope you'll keep coming. Dr. Graham means well, but I think a younger doctor like yourself is probably more up-to-date on modern medicine and would help to keep up Will's spirits.

Mr. Adams: Bertha, we can't impose on the doctor.

Dr. Dawson: Not at all. The ossification seems to be progressing rapidly so we need to keep an eye on it. Why don't I come back next week? That will give me time to do some research on how we might slow the disease's progress, and when I come back (smiling at Bertha), I'll be sure to stay for that tea.

Bertha: (smiling at him) Thank you, Doctor.

Dr. Dawson: (turning to retrieve his medical bag from the chair) Thank you, Mrs. Beard. I appreciate your confidence in me. And you also, Mr. Adams.

Mr. Adams: (shaking his hand) Thank you, Doctor.

[Dr. Dawson exits. As he leaves the room, Mrs. Adams enters with Norma.]

Mrs. Adams: Will, Norma is here to see you.

Bertha: Oh good, now we'll have a guest for tea after all. [But as she speaks, she goes to the porch to watch Dr. Dawson walk away from the house.]

Norma: Hello, Will.

Will: Hello, Norma. Did you come because you heard I was dying? Just because I intend to be a playwright doesn't mean you'll be getting any deathbed speeches out of me.

Mrs. Adams: (shocked) Will, what a thing to say!

Mr. Adams: (to Norma). It's good to see you again, Norma. (to Mrs. Adams) Come, Harriet. Let's leave the young people alone.

Mrs. Adams: I want to know what the doctor said.

Mr. Adams: Come into the parlor and I'll tell you.

[They exit.]

Norma: (sitting down beside him) Will, is it true that they don't expect you'll ever walk again?

Will: Yes, but I don't know that walking is all that it's cracked up to be anyway, and not everyone has ossified legs. Why, I bet I could get a job in the freak show if I just had a way to get there.

Norma: Will, you're terrible.

[Bertha returns from the porch, looking starry-eyed. She walks over to a chair but stares into space a moment and Will and Norma both notice.]

Norma: (to Bertha) Was that Dr. Dawson who was just here?

Bertha: Yes. Do you know him?

Norma: I thought it was him. He's very kind. He treated me when I had strep throat last winter.

Bertha: He does seem very kind, doesn't he, and don't you think he's handsome?

Will: What about the tea, Sister?

Bertha: Be patient, Will. Would you like some tea, Norma?

Norma: Yes, thank you, Mrs. Beard. That would be very nice.

[Bertha pours the tea and passes around the cups on saucers.]

Will: Bertha, please put my drawings where no one will spill tea on them.

Norma: Oh, what have you been drawing, Will?

Will: Why, I've been drawing the most remarkable creature that walks upon the face of this earth.

Norma: And what is that?

Will: Why, you must guess.

Norma: Okay, I'll guess. Is it a man-eating animal?

Will: You might say that.

Norma: Is it a lion?

Will: (considering) No, no, I wouldn't say that. I'm not sure it has courage so much as audacity.

Norma: Is it cunning?

Will: Very much so.

Norma: Does it have a lot of fur?

Will: Only on its chin, unless you count its winter coat.

Norma: Is it a goat?

Will: (laughing) No, but it might call its wife an old one.

Norma: Its wife? You mean its mate if it's an animal.

Will: No, I mean its wife.

Norma: (pondering a moment) Then it must be a human, Will. But you said it had fur.

Will: I said only on its chin and its winter coat.

Norma: Just show me the drawings. I give up.

Bertha: Here, Norma.

[Bertha passes the drawings to Norma.]

Will: (triumphantly) It's the savvy businessman!

Norma: Why it's Mr. Kaufman and Mr. White!

Will: It is indeed.

Norma: I didn't know you could draw so well, Will, and they're funny too, but why are you drawing them?

Will: If I'm to end up bedridden, I don't want to forget people's faces.

Bertha: You won't be bedridden. I told you father would find a way for you to go to church and other places.

Will: I don't need to go out. There are plenty of places I can visit within my very own mind.

Norma: (laughing) Oh, come on, Will.

Will: I mean it. I just envision a place in my mind and it's just like being there.

Bertha: Just ignore him, Norma. None of us understand him when he waxes philosophic.

Will: The power of the imagination can transport us to wherever we want to go. For example, today is a warm summer day, and there's nothing I would rather do than go swimming, so I just imagine myself doing it. I even wrote a poem about it.

Norma: Oh, will you read it to me, Will?

[Bertha hands him the poem from the drawing book.]

Will: Yes, I call it "Summertime in Marquette":

I've been swimmin' all over,
From Chocolay to Birch
In the place where the kids
Grab suckers and perch,
But there ain't no use talking
Th' daisiest shock
Is th' one that you get
Off Charley Gaines' rock.

Say I've done belly-floppers
And busted my ribs
In th' old cinder pond
And th' Grace furnace cribs.
Yit they'll do in a pinch
Fur I don't want to knock
But bets they ain't in it
With Charley Gaines' rock.

Norma: (clapping) That's wonderful, Will. I could see Gaines' Rock myself.

Will: See, Bertha. She does get it. I knew she was of superior intelligence.

Bertha: Well, I wish I had some of it. Then maybe I could imagine...(becoming starry-eyed as she speaks), but no, I think maybe now I'd rather.... Are you done with your tea, Norma? I'll clear these dishes away.

Norma: Yes, thank you.

[Bertha collects the cups and puts them on the tea tray while Will speaks.]

Will: Now see, Norma, I figure if I can't walk, it's because the Lord has other plans for me. He gave me this ailment so I could better focus on my real talents and my first love.

Bertha: (to herself) Or second....

Will: What?

Bertha: Nothing.

[Bertha gets up to collect the tea tray and exits as Norma and Will continue to speak.]

Norma: (hopeful about his response) Will, what do you mean by your first love?

Will: Literature. So long as I can still move my arms, I can write.

Norma: Are you writing anything now?

Will: Yes, I'm planning to launch a magazine called *CHIPS*. And any good magazine has cartoons, so I'll keep drawing, too. I might just be the next Charles Dickens—no point in not having great expectations.

Norma: But didn't Dickens die from overwork?

Will: Yes, at his desk, doing what he loved, but that's hardly as interesting as dying from ossification—will make me a downright literary curiosity someday. In the meantime, I'll be selling ads for my magazine to pay for its printing.

Norma: But, Will, how will you sell the ads if you're bedridden?

Will: Why, with the telephone. Anyone can do almost anything from anywhere because of that little wonder.

[A clock chimes five o'clock.]

Norma: I love hearing how you use your imagination to get around problems, Will. I wish I was so imaginative, but I better be getting home for supper now. Keep up your spirits.

Will: No fear of that, but there's one thing my imagination can't do.

Norma: What's that?

Will: Make you come visit me. You will come again soon, won't you?

Norma: I'll come every week, Will, if I won't be interfering with your magazine work.

Will: Not at all. You can bring me all the gossip to put in my society column.

Norma: (laughing) Oh, Will. I came to cheer you up, but I think you've cheered me up instead. Goodbye.

Will: Goodbye, Norma.

Gaines Rock, named for William Gaines, a former slave and the natural son of a white Virginia shipbuilder. He came to Marquette in 1855 and lived at Gaines Rock until his death in 1903. Gaines was a particular favorite with Marquette's children because he always carried pennies in one pocket and candy in another, both of which he liberally passed out. Will Adams may have been one of those beneficiaries. (Photo courtesy of Sonny Longtine)

Norma's House at 420 High Street

Interior of Norma's House. This image is taken from a 1960s magazine.

Scene 7: Norma's Apartment, 1963

[Boxes are mixed in among the living room furniture to suggest Norma is moving. Grace and Norma are sorting through old belongings and packing away new ones as they speak.]

Norma: Grace, I'm really grateful to you for staying a few extra days to help me move.

Grace: That's what sisters do, and besides, I think it's awful your landlord would even ask you to move.

Norma: Oh, I don't blame him. If I had a daughter who was moving back home, I'd want her to live near me also, and I really don't need all this space at my age.

Grace: Still, to throw an old lady out of her house.

Norma: Who's an old lady?

Grace: Considering the stuff you have around here, I'd say you are. You should give this stuff to Fred Rydholm. Didn't you tell me he's writing a book about Marquette? Or give it to the historical society; a lot of it looks like it belongs in a museum.

Norma: I suppose you think I should be in a museum, too.

Grace: If the shoe fits.... But look at this—it must be seventy years old!

[From a box, Grace pulls out the Valentine that Will gave Norma.]

Norma: (eyes lighting up when she sees it) Yes, it must be, though it's hard to imagine.

Grace: It must have been some lovesick boy who gave it to you. (reading it out loud)

> Miss Norma Ross,
> you can have your musical art.
> Just let me be the boss
> of your beautiful heart.
> Be my Valentine.
> W.S.

Who gave you this? I bet you don't even remember who W.S. was. He obviously didn't become a poet.

Norma: (reaching for it) Of course I know who W.S. was. Will Adams. He signed himself that way. S was for Sidney, his father's name and his middle name. And he was only a boy when he wrote that so you give him a break. You know he became a wonderful writer.

Grace: (looking apologetic) Oh, yes, Will. Funny, though. I thought you were the one who always pursued him.

Norma: (sort of softly) He gave this to me before he realized he was going to be paralyzed for life.

Grace: (looking away with embarrassment) What else do you have in here? Let's see. [She digs through the box and pulls out a copy of *CHIPS*.]

Norma: You remember that, don't you? Will's first magazine.

Grace: Oh, yes. I remember how thrilled you were when it first came out. You were as proud of Will as if you had written it yourself.

Norma: He was a remarkable young man. Imagine, publishing your first magazine at age seventeen.

Grace: I did enjoy reading it. I think even the people he lampooned enjoyed it. Remember the poem he wrote making fun of Ernie Ludlow's pants?

Norma: Let me see it. [Grace hands it to her.] This is the first issue. Oh, I remember. This is the one that got Dr. Dawson so discombobulated. I used to love hearing Will tell that story.

Grace: Discombobulated about what?

Masthead of an issue of *CHIPS*

Left: For much of her life, Norma Ross lived within view of the Adams House. Pictured here is her view of St. Paul's and the Adams House from her front yard on High Street, less than two blocks away.

Below: Norma spent her last years living in the Pine Ridge Apartments, a new high-rise apartment building for senior citizens constructed in the heart of Marquette's historical residential district, just a block east of the Adams home.

![Pine Ridge Apartments building]

Scene 8: The Adams House, 1895

[Dr. Dawson is closing up his medical bag after examining Will.]

Will: For two years now, Doctor, you've been coming here, and I know someone who appreciates it very much.

Dr. Dawson: I'm happy to do it, Will. I just wish I knew better how to help you.

Will: I'm not talking about me, Doctor.

Dr. Dawson: Oh, well, your parents are very kind I'm sure.

Will: I'm not talking about them either.

Dr. Dawson: (blushing, embarrassed) Well, now. Your father told me after the examination to come see him about my bill, if you'll excuse me.

Will: (laughing) Your red face tells what your tongue won't, Doctor.

[Dr. Dawson starts to exit when Bertha enters carrying a newspaper in her hand.]

Bertha: (sort of stopped in her tracks) Hello, James, um, Dr. Dawson.

Dr. Dawson: (slightly bowing) Mrs. Beard.

[He exits and Bertha, remembering why she entered, rushes over to Will.]

Bertha: Will, it's here—the first issue of *CHIPS*. It's so exciting. To think you're a newspaper editor at seventeen!

[Will gleefully pages through the paper. The screen shows the cover and various pages of *CHIPS* as he turns them.]

Will: I'm glad to see it. I'm quite impressed by myself.

Bertha: Oh, it's beautiful, Will. I love the cartoons and everything you wrote for it is so witty.

Will: True, true, but I fear people will not read it for its literary gems but the gossip.

Bertha: What do you mean?

Will: Well, it's bad enough to have a society column, but then the letters to the editors I received— they're like personal ads. But I printed them anyway since I was short on copy.

Bertha: What do the letters say?

Will: Oh, they're just anonymous love poems and other such mush.

Bertha: Oh, that's terrible. Who would want their love to be made public like that?

Will: (smiling to himself) You'd be surprised, Sister. [He pages through the paper until he finds what he's looking for.] Take a look. Right here is a good example.

[Bertha stands beside him, reading it over his shoulder as he reads aloud. Her eyes grow wider and wider as he reads.]

To a Certain Young Widow

Ma'am, some say I'm a quack

But I've cared for your brother,

And been respectful to your mother,

So I hope you won't give me no flack.

I can't say I've saved your brother's life.

Or that between us there'd never be strife.

But if you'd become my wife.

I promise you'll ride in a most handsome hack.

Bertha: Oh, no!

Will: I know. Pretty awful, isn't it? I mean, it doesn't even follow a standard rhyme scheme and it has no sense of meter at all.

Bertha: But, Will, don't you see?

Will: See what?

Bertha: Why, it's about me...me and Dr.—

[Dr. Dawson reenters the room.]

Dr. Dawson: Will, I forgot to leave you these sleeping pills.

Will: Sleeping pills...oh, right. What's in them?

Dr. Dawson: Just a little morphine to ease your pain so you get a good night's rest.

Will: Well, I'm glad someone will get a good night's rest in this house. I don't imagine Bertha will.

Dr. Dawson: (looking at her in confusion) Why, what's wrong, Mrs. Beard?

Will: It seems something in the paper has upset her.

Dr. Dawson: What is it?

Bertha: Oh, I wouldn't say "upset."

Will: Show it to the good doctor, Sister.

[She reluctantly allows Dr. Dawson to take the paper from her.]

Bertha: Will, I'm sure he...already knows....

Dr. Dawson: What is it? (scanning the pages until he sees it) Good heavens! Mrs. Beard, I—I didn't—

Bertha: (starting to glow) You don't have to apologize, Doctor. I know you didn't mean to embarrass me. It's rather romantic actually. It's just—

Will: It's just that she prefers her proposals on bended knee.

Bertha: Oh, no, it's just that I didn't know you felt the same way I do.

Dr. Dawson: (jubilant, trying to restrain his emotion) You do! [He takes her hand in his, then looks like he fears he's being too forward.]

Bertha: (laughing) Yes, ever since the first day you came. Oh, I didn't think you could love a widow, but....

Dr. Dawson: But I do. I do.

[Mrs. Adams enters.]

Mrs. Adams: What's all the excitement?

Will: (to his mother) Don't you hear the bells?

Mrs. Adams: What bells?

Will: Wedding bells.

[Mrs. Adams looks confused until Bertha explains.]

Bertha: Mother, Dr. Dawson has proposed to me, and I've said, "Yes."

[Dr. Dawson looks relieved, then confused.]

Mrs. Adams: (smiling) And how did this finally come about? Tell me all the details.

Bertha: Just look at what he printed in the paper. [She hands the copy of *CHIPS* to her mother.]

Dr. Dawson: (confused) But I don't understand. I—I—didn't write that.

Bertha: (wide-eyed and looking at him) You didn't? Then, who...?

[Everyone turns at once and looks at Will.]

Will: (smirking with glee) It helps to have a newspaper man in the family, doesn't it, Doctor?

James and Bertha Dawson were happily married, and according to Clyde Steele in *It Seems Like Yesterday*, they were perfectly suited for each other. Steele, who personally knew Dr. Dawson, goes on to state:

"In 1926 the good doctor, while in Hollywood, California, purchased a motorhome which had belonged to Douglas Fairbanks and Mary Pickford....

Childs Art Gallery MARQUETTE, MICH.

"Having amassed a fortune he retired from his profession quite early and he and his beloved wife Bertha traveled extensively. They had a residence in Pomono, Calif., where they usually spent part of the winter months and in the summer they frequented Marquette.

"Disaster struck when Bertha became ill and she was confined to her bed a lengthy period of time before passing away. Life was never the same for the doctor although he traveled extensively but never returned to places where he and Bertha had previously visited. His wife Bertha was 61 at the time of her death."

Scene 9: The Adams House, 1896

[Will is in bed, holding the telephone receiver to his ear with his left hand. Dr. Dawson is holding the telephone's base for him.]

Will: Hello, Mr. Reinhardt. Will S. Adams, Manufacturer & Dealer in Literary Junk here. I'm just calling to make sure you'll be taking out an ad in *CHIPS* this month because not to do so would be a great loss to your business. You don't want your competitors scooping up your profits.

[Will pauses to listen.]

Will: A fair point indeed, sir, but the good Dr. Dawson is here with me, and he will assure you that to every new subscriber a tombstone epitaph will be given. I write them myself. You know my publication specializes in obituaries.

[Will pauses to listen.]

Will: Why, that's why I have the good doctor here to assist me. Who better to help me oversee the writing of obituaries than Dr. Dawson?

[Will pauses to listen as Dr. Dawson smiles and shakes his head in amusement.]

Will: What's that? You don't want an ad? Why, that's probably the best way to get your obituary in my publication. I'll make sure there's one for Reinhardt Groceries in the next issue since no doubt your failure to place an ad in *CHIPS* will result in your business' sudden demise.

[Will pauses to listen.]

Will: Thank you, sir. It's a pleasure doing business with you, regardless.

[He hands the receiver to Dr. Dawson to hang up the telephone.]

Will: That was a lost cause, but it's his loss. I can't be the economic savior of every business in Marquette, you know.

Dr. Dawson: No, I guess not, Will.

Will: Well, I thank you for your help, Doctor. It's such a shame my right arm has stiffened up so much I can't lift it to hold the telephone now. I wonder how much longer before I lose the use of the other one.

Dr. Dawson: I'm afraid it won't be long now, Will. A few months if you're lucky. But I suspect you have many years ahead of you, regardless.

Will: Still, I don't know what I'll do once you and my sister go off to California for the winter. You've literally become my right-hand man.

Dr. Dawson: (smiling) I wish you could come with us, Will, but I hesitate to move you that far.

Will: I can't go anyway when I have a magazine to publish.

[The telephone rings. Dr. Dawson picks it up and puts it beside Will's ear.]

Will: W.S. Adams, esquire, proprietor of literary junk, and editor-in-chief of *CHIPS* magazine.

[As Will pauses to listen, Norma enters.]

Will: Very good, Mr. Reinhardt. I knew you were a discerning connoisseur of the almighty magazine advertisement. I'll have a copy of the ad brought to you next week for approval.

[Will pauses to listen.]

Will: Yes, sir.

[Will pauses to listen.]

Will: Yes, sir.

[Will pauses to listen.]

Will: Yes, sir, and if you ever do carry clams at your store, please let me know because I'd like to purchase some to clam certain people's mouths shut. Good day, sir.

[Dr. Dawson hangs up the telephone. Norma is smirking.]

Will: Hello, Norma. To what do I owe this pleasure? Are you here to say goodbye to the Doctor and Bertha? You know they're going to California next week.

Norma: I hope you have a pleasant trip, Doctor. I know everyone in Marquette will miss you.

Dr. Dawson: Thank you, Norma. I'll miss all of you as well.

Norma: Will, I actually came to tell you I'll also be leaving Marquette for a while.

Will: Leave Marquette!

Norma: Yes, this afternoon actually.

Dr. Dawson: Excuse me. I promised to help Bertha with the packing.

[Dr. Dawson exits. Norma takes his chair beside Will's bed.]

Will: So where are you going?

Norma: To study music at Northwestern University so I can become a music teacher. I was accepted there weeks ago, but I didn't know how to tell you. I was afraid you'd be disappointed.

Will: (trying to hide his disappointment) Oh, well now, that's what you've always wanted, so I wish you much luck. When you get back to town and start giving singing lessons, let me know and I'll give you a special rate on an ad in *CHIPS*.

Norma: That's kind of you, Will, but I'm hoping to get a job as a schoolteacher rather than give private lessons.

Will: Well, I wish you much luck. Now if you'll excuse me, a long day of selling ads has me quite tuckered out.

Norma: Will, don't take a nap yet. I came special to see you and say goodbye.

Will: Well, I'm glad you're going away to school. You should have gone last year. You're just wasting your time constantly coming over here.

Norma: Will, what do you mean?

Will: Why, you're the Belle of Marquette. Didn't the *Mining Journal*'s popularity poll determine you were the most popular young person in the city? Why waste your time coming to see me with that voice of yours and all the young men whose hearts you're breaking because you won't give them the time of day.

Norma: Whose heart am I breaking?

Will: Lots of young men's.

Norma: Name one.

Will: If I started naming names, we'd be here all day.

Norma: Will, most of the young men only think about how much money they can make or how much fun they want to have, but not one of them has anything of substance to talk about, much less your sense of humor.

Will: What about that Ernie Ludlow? He and you have some common interests in the theatre.

Norma: You can't be serious. Have you seen those crazy pants he wears?

Will: Because he's trying to get your attention. And he has two good legs to take a girl dancing and two strong arms for holding a woman. And so do plenty of other young men who are interested in you.

Norma: But not one of them can sing like you.

Will: What good is my singing? I can't perform anymore. Not when I'm stuck in this bed.

Norma: Don't say you're stuck, Will. I don't like to hear you sound down.

Will: No, what I mean is if I were meant to sing, God would have made it possible for me. Writing I can do at home, but singing needs to be done in public.

Norma: That may be, but it's a shame because you have such a beautiful voice.

Will: It's nothing compared to yours. I don't know what you want to be a music teacher for. You should follow your dream to be an opera singer.

Norma: Oh, I don't think my voice is good enough.

Will: Are you kidding me? Why, I'm sure if the young men of Paris heard you, they'd unhook the horses from your carriage and pull it through the streets themselves.

Norma: I'd like to see that happen. You make it sound so vivid, Will. You should write an opera and make that one of the scenes.

Will: Yes, I should, and then you could star in it.

Norma: Maybe someday, but I really just want to come back to Marquette to teach.

Will: And never let that beautiful voice be heard by the world?

Norma: Will, I don't care about fame. I've never aspired to being the next Shakespeare like you have, and I just want to be in Marquette and near....

[An awkward silent moment follows. Will changes the subject.]

Will: Hand me that telephone, will you? I have to call back that grocer.

[Norma hands Will the receiver and holds the telephone base for him.]

Will: Hello, Mr. Reinhardt. I've decided I'm going to give you a special deal, an even bigger ad at no extra cost, just to prove to you how much I believe in my publication.

[Will pauses to listen.]

Will: Yes, sir, I promise you won't be disappointed. Why *CHIPS* is the finest magazine in the entire Great Lakes region. Puts that mining rag to shame, it does. I guarantee you'll see a boost in your sales from the ad I create for you.

[As Will is talking, Dr. Dawson returns.]

Norma: (whispering) Doctor, I have to be going.

[Dr. Dawson takes the telephone from Norma while Will listens. For a moment, Will pulls away from the telephone, like he wants to speak to her.]

Norma: I have to go, Will. My train leaves in a couple of hours.

Will: (nodding as he speaks to the grocer) All right, of course we can mention that you'll have a special sale on melons all month.

[Norma exits.]

Will: Thank you, Mr. Reinhardt. You have a good day, sir.

[Dr. Dawson takes away the telephone.]

Dr. Dawson: Well, I better get back to the packing.

[Will nods as Dr. Dawson exits.]

Will: I don't know why Norma had to rush off like that. I was almost off the telephone. [He's silent for a minute.] Well, she'll write, I'm sure. If only I could write her a song so the opera houses would notice her, maybe have her record it for the phonograph even....

[He begins humming the opening bars to "You Will Not Love Me."]

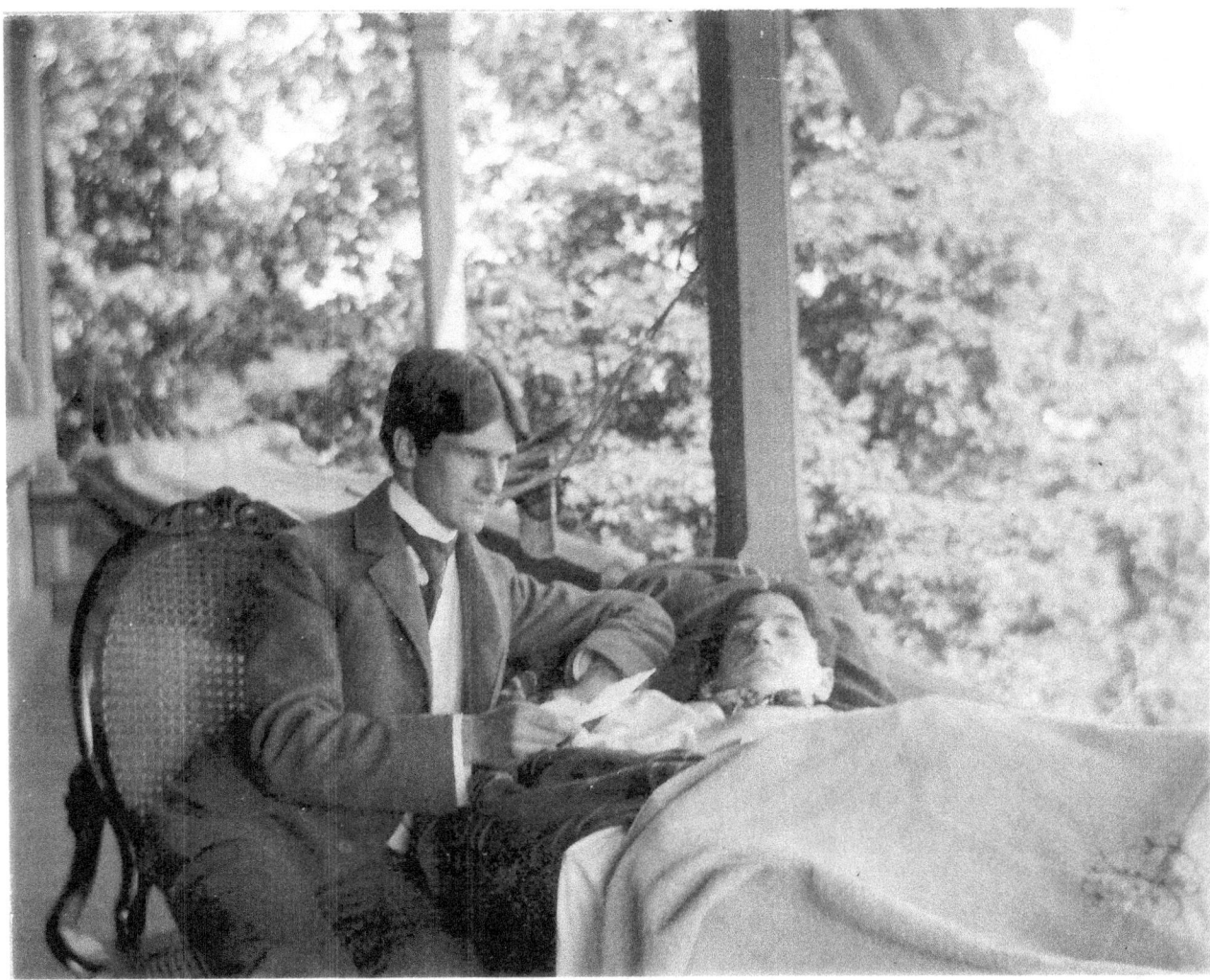

Just as Dr. Dawson holds the telephone for Will in the play, so Will had a secretary and other attendants to assist him. Here he is with one of his attendants whose name has been lost.

Scene 10: The Adams House, 1900

[Will alone, looking glum in his bed. There is a newspaper and a cigar box on the table beside him. Norma enters. At first, he doesn't see her and she gazes upon him; then unable to control herself, she rushes to his side.]

Norma: Will!

Will: (startled but pleased) Norma! Why! My goodness! I knew you were coming home, but you didn't say in your last letter what day.

Norma: I know, Will. Things were just hectic the last few days before I left. I was meaning to write, but well...

Will: "Well" what?

Norma: Oh, it doesn't matter now. It's just...I had a difficult decision to make and—

Will: It's that college boy you wrote me about.

Norma: It's nothing, Will.

Will: It is. I knew he had designs on you. I was right, wasn't I? I suppose you're going to marry him. Hand me a cigar, will you? I think I'm going to need it.

[Norma hands him a cigar from beside the bed and lights it for him.]

Will: (talking with the cigar in his mouth) So, are you? Are you going to marry him?

Norma: He...he did propose to me.

Will: I knew it! Of course, he must be the smartest man at that university to set his eyes on you. Not that I'm surprised. I mean, those boys never before saw a northern rose from Lake Superior's shore. I'm surprised you didn't have to swat them all off like mosquitoes. So when's the wedding?

[As Will speaks, Norma grabs an ashtray to hold beneath Will's cigar.]

Norma: There...there isn't going to be a wedding. I told him, "No."

[Will's mouth drops open and the cigar falls into the ashtray.]

Norma: (setting aside the ashtray) Will, you're going to burn the house down. I'm surprised your family lets you smoke at all. What does the Doctor say?

Will: When your doctor's your brother-in-law, he knows better than to tell you what to do.

Norma: Yes, but Dr. Dawson is in California now. What does your doctor in Marquette say?

Will: What's he going to say? I told him smoking relieves the tension for me, and he smokes like a chimney himself. Anyway, I won't ask why you broke that young man's heart, but just remember, there are plenty of trees in the forest.

Norma: Never mind, Will. Tell me how you've been? How is *CHIPS* doing?

Will: Oh, well enough, but I've delegated a lot of the work to my staff and other writers now so I can explore other literary avenues. If I don't look for fresh ideas and projects, the writing will grow stale you know.

Norma: So what will your next project be?

Will: I haven't exactly decided, but now that you're here, I'm sure you'll help to inspire me. You will come to see me regularly again now that you're home?

Norma: Yes, although I do need to find a teaching position.

Will: I'm sure that won't be a problem. With all the people your father and mine know, someone will help you.

Norma: But I want to succeed on my own merits, Will.

Will: You mean you don't want anyone helping you out because you're a woman.

Norma: Exactly.

Will: That's my girl. You shouldn't expect anyone to do things for you. No one wants to be pitied; that's for sure.

Norma: I'm glad you understand, Will. That's part of why I said, "No" to the proposal. He wanted me to stay home and raise a family, but then, what would have been the point of my going to school all these years? So I told him, "No, thank you. I'll have plenty of children when I teach."

Will: Why, he sounds like a positive Neanderthal!

Norma: Oh, he was nice enough, just not nice enough for me, I guess.

Will: I'm surprised he didn't want you to work while he stayed home with the kids. Seems some of the men these days are willing to sponge off the women. At least these English lords I've been reading about in the newspaper are. Where is that rag? Mother got called away before she could finish reading it to me. Would you finish it for me?

[Norma retrieves the newspaper and opens it.]

Norma: What did you want me to read?

Will: There was some story about a milksop duke getting engaged.

Norma: Oh, here it is. "The announcement from London of the Duke of Roxburghe and Miss May Goelet was confirmed today by the prospective bride's mother. The prospective groom is Sir Henry John Innes-Ker, Duke of Roxburghe, Marquis of Bowmont and Cessford, and Baron Ker of Cessford and Cavertoun in Scotland.... The present fortune of Miss Goelet is estimated at about twenty million dollars."

Will: Twenty million all to become the property of some English lord! Why, it's robbing America! It's like the Brits are trying to make up for those taxes we didn't pay at the Boston Tea Party.

Norma: Oh, Will. You're so cynical.

Will: Cynical? Didn't we break from Britain to get away from all those lords and their fancy titles, but now our young ladies are running after them.

Norma: I don't think you can blame a young lady for wanting a little romance in her life.

Will: Romance? How would you like a man to love you only for your money?

Norma: I haven't any money, so it doesn't matter.

Will: But it's the principle of the thing.

Norma: It still wouldn't matter because I wouldn't marry unless the right man asked me.

Will: But what if he didn't? Would you settle for someone else?

Norma: Why wouldn't he ask me?

Will: Oh, I'm sure he'd have his reasons, but I mean, you wouldn't never want to get married.

Norma: I don't need to be married. I'd just devote myself to my music and teaching. Don't you think that would be a fulfilling enough life?

Will: Maybe for a man, not a woman.

Norma: I don't see why not.

Will: (frowning) A man can get by without love in his life, especially if he doesn't think he can make a woman happy. He'd be a cad to marry a woman he knew he couldn't make happy.

Norma: But, Will, how would he know what a woman—

[Mrs. Adams enters.]

Mrs. Adams: Hello, Norma. I see you're back from school. We're all so proud of you.

Norma: Thank you.

Mrs. Adams: I was just coming to bring Will in for supper. Will you stay to eat with us?

Norma: Oh, thank you, but no. My family would be upset if I weren't home for supper my first night back in Marquette. I should be going. Goodbye, Will.

Will: But we barely had a visit. You'll come tomorrow, won't you?

Norma: Yes, I promise.

Mrs. Adams: I'll walk you out, Norma. Will, I'll be back for you in a minute.

[Will's eyes follow Norma as she and his mother leave the room. After they are gone, he sighs, but after a moment, his face lights up as he talks.]

Will: Craziness. Plumb craziness. I imagine Miss Goelet has had plenty of American men after her money, but I guess the title is what did it for her. Still, what a reason to marry. Downright silly. Someone should write a comic song about it—no, I should write a comic song about it! Or maybe...maybe I could....

Scene 11: The Adams House, 1903

[Will is humming "You Will Not Love Me" when Norma enters.]

Norma: Hello, Will.

Will: Aha! Just the person I wanted to see!

Norma: You're in a chipper mood today. What was that you were humming?

Will: Do you like it?

Norma: Yes, very much, but I never heard it before.

Will: It's new.

Norma: New? I don't recognize it. Is it from a new Victor Herbert show?

Will: (laughing) No, and you know my taste runs more toward Gilbert and Sullivan.

Norma: But Sullivan is dead, so it can't be one of theirs. It sounds sad. Too sad for George M. Cohan.

Will: I wouldn't say it's completely sad, but you're getting closer.

Norma: Oh, Will. I don't know. Just tell me.

Will: All right. You wouldn't have guessed anyway because you've never heard an original operetta score by this composer.

Norma: Is it from a show?

Will: It is from the upcoming operetta *Miss D.Q. Pons.*

Norma: That's a funny name for a show. Who wrote it?

Will: It's the ingenious invention of the three-hatted playwright, composer, and lyricist, W.S. Adams, Esquire; in other words, yours truly, my dear.

Norma: Oh, Will, stop your kidding.

Will: I assure you I kid not. I'm writing it myself, but it's all in my head right now, so I need you to help me put the music down on paper before I forget it all.

Norma: Why, you're serious!

Will: Very serious. I've already got six songs for the show in my head and the dialogue for the full first act, and it's just bursting to come out of me, but I can't trust Mother or Father to help me write it down because they do not have adequate musical talent. However, I understand you're well-qualified, Miss Bachelorette of Music, or should I say "Miss D.Q. Pons."

Norma: Will, you never cease to astound me...but what do you mean by calling me Miss D.Q. Pons?

Will: I mean that I intend for you to be the star of the show.

Norma: Oh, Will. I—

Will: Don't go being bashful, Norma. You have a beautiful voice, and you know you love the theatre, and besides, you don't even know what the show is about yet.

Norma: That's true, but knowing you, I can guess it'll be a comedy.

Will: Absolutely. Now, remember when I was complaining about that heiress marrying an English lord?

Norma: Yes...

Will: Well, I couldn't stop thinking about it, so I based the whole operetta on it, and I stayed up half the night envisioning it in my mind. It's going to be a grand production like nothing the Marquette Opera House ever saw, and—

Norma: You mean you plan to write and produce it?

Will: My dear, what's the point of writing an operetta if no one is to see it? Now, are you going to help me? I'm already afraid I'm starting to forget the lyrics I wrote for Lord Breakus.

Norma: Yes, I'll help. I assume Lord Breakus is the suitor vying for Miss D.Q. Pons' hand?

Will: Oh, yes, but he's just one of Miss D.Q. Pons' many suitors. There's also a colonel. After all, she's an American heiress and a belle, so she can have any man she wants.

Norma: (thoughtfully) But maybe she doesn't want just any man.

Will: Precisely. And that, Norma, is why you are perfect for playing the title role.

Norma: I don't know that I understand.

Will: You wouldn't settle for just any man, would you, my dear, and besides, who else in Marquette has the talent to pull off the role? You'll be putting Lillian Russell to shame by the time I feature you in this play.

Norma: Oh, I'm no Lillian Russell.

Will: Of course not. She's a beautiful woman, but she doesn't have your figure. She's only such a big star because you haven't been discovered yet. That's why you need me.

Norma: You're going to get me discovered?

Will: Norma, I intend to make you a star. I'll be your Svengali.

[Will gives Norma a hypnotic leer in true Svengali style.]

Norma: Oh, don't say that. That story gives me the creeps.

Will: All right, but *Miss D.Q. Pons* will make you a star nevertheless. Now, sit at the piano over there and we'll start. I'll hum and sing the lyrics for you, and you write down the notes, all right?

Norma: Very well.

Will: Let's begin with your big song. I haven't figured out the lyrics for it yet, but here's the melody.

[Norma seats herself at the piano. Will begins to hum "You Will Not Love Me."]

Norma: Wait. I need a pencil and some blank sheet music to write on.

Will: Look in the piano bench.

[Norma does so as she speaks.]

Norma: I hope you won't be disappointed in me, Will. I can sing, but I've never acted.

Will: Disappointment can only come from not making the effort. Now, do you want to be the next Lillian Russell or not?

[By now, Norma has the sheet music and pencil and reseats herself at the piano.]

Norma: (looking a bit starry eyed) Do you think—

Will: (cutting her off) Get that pencil ready. Here it comes. Next thing you know, *Miss D.Q. Pons* will be on stage at the Marquette Opera House. [He starts humming again.]

Plays- 394

FIFTH PRESENTATION OF

Miss D. Q. Pons

 An Original Comic Opera
BY
Will S. Adams and Norma Ross

PRESENTED:

MARQUETTE........July 3rd	SAULT STE. MARIE..Dec. 1st
ISHPEMING.........July 18th	MARQUETTE.......Dec. 8th
MARQUETTE........July 20th	CHICAGO..........?

Cover of the original *Miss D.Q. Pons* program

MARQUETTE OPERA HOUSE,
MARQUETTE, MICH.

Albert F. Koepcke,
Manager.

Monday, July 3rd, 1905.

Initial Performance of

"MISS D. Q. PONS"

An Original Comic Opera.

Words, Lyrics and Music by WILL S. ADAMS and NORMA ROSS   Piano Arrangement, - - NORMA ROSS
Orchestration, - - - - FRANK TROMBLEY

CAST OF CHARACTERS.

Mozart Grabenheimer (Graham White), leader of the
157th regiment band from Wienersberg on the Rind..
....Roy Young
Rubenstein Bockspeer (Arthur Digby), cymbal expert
and member of Brass Jammers' union...........Al Shauer
Tipperary McGinnis O'Toole (alias Tip), orderly to Lord
Westinghouse Breakus.....................Bernie Goodman
Lord Westinghouse Breakus, an English general and
gentleman of quality—in America on tour of inspec-
tion of United States army...................T. E. Ludlow
Rubber-tired Willie, a ragged beam of sunshine spread-
ing happiness while in quest of a long lost love (miss-
ing three days) ....Will A. Ross

Sammy Sloane, a messenger boy and distant relative of
Todd Sloane............. .... Earl Ross
Colonel Jack Foster, a military man who is in love with
Miss D. Q Pons........................ Dr. Eldred Robbins
Miss D. Q. Pons, a true American girl, and only daughter
of a billionaire ....Miss Norma Ross
Miss Hope To Be, a charming native of U. S., suffering
with Anglo-Mania and Titleitis—in love with Lord
Breakus...........................Miss Flora Retallic
Miss Cyanide DePotassium, an actress on her summer
vacation—not a show girl, remember, but one of the
profesh, and always ready to flirt.........Miss Grace Cook
Miss Daisy Montgomery, the unknown girl..Miss Agnes Withey

Stage Direction, - - - W. A. ROSS	Properties, - - - PHIL. ROSE
Business Manager, - - SELDEN B. CRARY	Electrician, - - - CHAS. RETALLIC
Advance Agent, - - HARRY F. BENDING	Calcium, - - - LOUIS GENETT

The original cast of *Miss D.Q. Pons* from the program

SYNOPSIS.

ACT I.

Scene: Pavilion, Siesta-by-the-Sea. Time—July 3, 1905.

Twenty-four charming boys and girls will sing "O, What Joy."—Biff! Bang! Bang! It's Rubber Tired Willie.—Listen! He is going to sing "Memories."—What! It's little Sammy Sloane with a telegram. Certainly, Sammy will sing "The Messenger Boy."—Behold the lady with titleitis! Listen carefully to what she has to say to Lord Breakus, and don't overlook the recitation "Dreams," by Rubber Tired Willie.—That last song by Miss Hope To Be was "My Dream's Come True!"—Ah, 'tis the funny page of the Chicago American that approaches.—It's Lord Breakus and Tipperary McGinnis O'Toole.—Lord Breakus will now tell us in song why we are "So Hasty."—Rah! Rah! It's Miss D. Q. Pons. Hark! She's going to sing "When I Go A-Strolling."—Lord Breakus has grown tired (He is thinking of the 4th)—So the double quartet will sing "Mother's Lullaby."—'Tis Cyanide, full of ennui and histrionic ability (A warm reunion).—The bugle call indicates the approach of Colonel Foster.—With the assistance of the resorters he will sing "The Military Man."—Miss Hope To Be hears from papa, while the chorus sings "Siesta-by-the-Sea."

SYNOPSIS.

ACT II.

Scene: Garden of Miss D. Q. Pons' Summer Cottage. Time—Evening.

Lord Breakus wishes he had more money—(He isn't the only one).—Tipperary announces his matrimonial intentions, and gives voice to the beautiful ballad "When Old Ireland's Free."—Hail to John Philip Sousa, with his peerless band!—This is the only place in the opera where outside melody is employed.—Get under the Annhauser-Bush, if you can, while Mozart and Rubenstein sing "Water's the Thing for me"—(Sans Creosote)—R. T. Willie will now reveal his identity, while the orchestra plays "Daisy."—It's exacting, but Miss D. Q. Pons extracts a promise and explains the meaning of "True Love." Well! If Miss Hope To Be hasn't arrived!—Lord Breakus will be along soon. looking for a rise in wheat (hardly).—Never mind; let him have your attention while he gives vent to a little song, "A Son of Uncle Sam" (Couldn't select a better time, could he?)—Arthur Digby will now tell what he knows about "Taxation Without Representation."—Here's where Miss D. Q. Pons and Colonel Foster have an understanding, and really admit that "Cupid Is Wise."—The guests are here.—Now for the quartet, "Isn't It Strange How People Change" (You change yourself, don't you, occasionally)—Tip hears the sad news, and takes over an Irish castle.—Winthrop Rogers fulfills his promise and finds the lady of his choice, who kindly informs the happy guest when it is time to love, assisted by the Siestaites in the musical gem "When the Moon Is Softly Beaming."—Wholesale engagement announcement is the next attraction before the young ladies and gentlemen express their feelings in the finale. "O, What Joy."

The Synopsis of the play from the original program

One of the original ads pages from the program

INTERMISSION

[During Intermission, the ads from the original *Miss D.Q. Pons* program are shown on screen.

A good piece of savory meat is half the meal. When the wise house-keeper goes marketing she remembers this, and drops in at
HATHWAY'S.

A Horse for $1.50.
For further particulars go to
Freeman Bros. Livery.

After the Opera,
Prince
has arranged to serve the patrons of *Miss D.Q. Pons* either to a dainty lunch or to a delightful dish of cooling Ice Cream. Everybody always visits the dispenser of eatables at the conclusion of a first night's production. Prince waits to serve you.

Here is a Tip Right Off the Iron.
It's a hot one. Buy your Meats and Groceries from
Gust Ericsson.
He's not a billionaire like Miss D.Q. Pons' Pa. That's no reason why you shouldn't patronize him, is it?

Did you ever see an Automobile with four legs?
We rent them, under the following guarantee: Never buck on a hill; never stop ten miles from town; never use gasoline or never explode. Call and look over our stock.
Stewart's Livery,
BARAGA AVENUE. MARQUETTE, MICH.

Marquette, Mich., July 3.
To the Audience:
The last time I was in Marquette I stopped with John Lewis at the Hotel Marquette. I have tried the Waldorf Astoria of New York, the Cecil of London, and the Auditorium of Chicago, but to tell the honest plain, every-day truth, leaving out the French on the bill of fare, John can beat them by four aces and a king.
Mr. D.Q. Pons

Sanitary Plumbing
ENOUGH SAID.
E.J. SINK.

Vandenboom's Dairy Milk
is the kind they use at "Siesta-by-the-Sea." By special request, however, Mr. Vandenboom will furnish the people of the city of Marquette with the same excellent quality. It will do you good to see our new drove of Gurnsey cattle, just imported from Wisconsin.
F.H. Vandenboom.

A MIDSUMMER
CLOSING OUT SALE.
Suits and Jackets at unheard of low prices. Our store will be a bargain hunter's paradise for the next two weeks. When you call, inspect our new department of Trunks, Suit Cases, Grips and Valises.
LOUIS GETZ.

O yes, we have
the Clothes!
Look around the Opera House at the well dressed people. The chances are the goods came from The Hub. This store is the center of style and fashion for men's wearing apparel. We carry a complete stock of Gents' Furnishing Goods, and defy competition in price where quality is considered.
The Hub,
WASHINGTON STREET.

Handy! O Yes!
A drug store that can furnish you with anything necessary quicker than you can tell what you want. The patrons of *Miss D.Q. Pons* must pass us. We will pass our patrons one hundred cents' worth of goods on every dollar. You know us, and we are only too pleased to know you. Walk in and walk away with some of our stock. No extra charge for satisfaction.
PEOPLE'S DRUG STORE.

Check, Please!
We will exchange it at the conclusion of *Miss D.Q. Pons*. Candy, Cigars, or a little gambol on the green. You know Aniba. He's right on your way home.
Aniba.

YOU NEED THE MONEY; WE KNEAD THE DOUGH.
Everyone needs something, more or less. There is nothing like knowing where to get it when you want it. Our Bakery supplies everything in the bread line. We don't give it away exactly, but make as moderate a price on it as possible.
Try our Cakes and Pastries. Sold exclusively at Siesta-by-the-Sea and Marquette.
A. CAMERON
THIRD STREET.

O for a dish of ice cream that makes
Your lips go smickity, smack, and takes
The glow from out your inner works
Where your ice cream appetite shyly lurks,
and cries aloud with a ravenous shout,
"It's STAFFORD'S for me when the show lets out."
Ask for the "D.Q. Pons" brand. It's a cooler from Coolersville.

This man lived to be 106 years old on Reinhardt's groceries.
Moral: Do likewise and live to enjoy your great grandchildren.
Robt. Reinhardt,
The Grocer.
SOUTH MARQUETTE

The originals of these last two ads in the *Miss. D.Q. Pons* program are on page 58.

Announcement in *The Daily Mining Journal*, July 12, 1905. One of Will Adams' many ads leading up to the night of the play:

CONCERNING
"MISS D. Q. PONS"

————

One Day Before the Opera

————

There are a few seats left. From recent measurements they are just your size. Have the management mark them off and don't procrastinate. (Did you notice the last word?)

Why is Miss D. Q. Pons like one of Jaedecke's cigars? The answer is simple—it draws well.

Why is the opening chorus, "Oh, What Joy," in Miss D. Q. Pons like the Northwestern railroad track? A. It is just like getting money from home. (The tramp, Rubber-Tired Willie, has to follow it.)

Why is Lord Breakus' monocle like a glass of brandy and soda in the morning? (Don't guess, ladies—it's an eye-opener.)

If it took the Dutch band in Miss D. Q. Pons three months to learn one tune, how long will it take the Light Guard and City bands to play together the little ditty Comrades? A. Don't ask foolish questions.

Why is Lord Breakus' monocle like a glass of brandy and soda in the morning? (Don't guess, ladies—it's an eye-opener.)

If it took the Dutch band in Miss D. Q. Pons three months to learn one tune, how long will it take the Light Guard and City bands to play together the little ditty Comrades? A. Don't ask foolish questions.

If it takes Miss Hope to Be two hours and a half to capture an English lord, how long will it take a man in the city jail to see his friends? A. Ten days.

Two little birds who wanted to see Miss D. Q. Pons were fighting over a ticket they found on Cleveland avenue. Said the first: "You sassy thing, you're Robbin me." "That's nothing," the second replied. "I guess you will have to Swallow it."

What's the difference between a box on the ear and a box at the opera Miss D. Q. Pons? A. The first affects the ear drum; if you try the other you will expect to hear some.

Good morning.

ACT II

Scene 1: Norma's Apartment, 1963

[Fred Rydholm and Norma Ross are sitting in her apartment having tea.]

Fred: Thanks for having me over, Miss Ross.

Norma: Fred, you're old enough to call me Norma now.

Fred: All right...Norma. And congratulations again on the award. It made me remember your connection to the Adams family, so I was hoping you could tell me something about them for the book I'm writing.

Norma: I'll be happy to tell you whatever I can that helps.

Fred: Do I remember hearing from someone that you and Will Adams once wrote an operetta together?

Norma: (looking nostalgic) Oh, yes. That was quite a long time ago, though.

Fred: What was it about?

Norma: Oh, it was about an American heiress who married an English lord. The typical silly operetta plot of those days.

Fred: I bet it was wonderful, though.

Norma: Will and I thought so, at least, and the audiences did. It ended up touring all over Upper Michigan.

Fred: I wish I could have heard it. I don't suppose you could sing any of it for me.

Norma: I think I remember a little of it. Let's see. There was a love song in it, or was that the song that was cut. Give me a minute and it will come back to me....

[She begins to sing.]

Norma: You will not love me. You won't say why.

Scene 2: The Adams House, June 1905

[Will is lying in his bed. Norma is sitting beside him reading over the script of *Miss D.Q. Pons*. A Southern colonel's hat and a Napoleon-style hat are lying on the sofa.]

Will: Norma, before the others get here, I thought I should tell you I decided not to include the love song in the operetta.

Norma: Oh, Will, but it's so beautiful.

Will: I know, but I just can't seem to find the right lyrics to go with it, and it's sort of a romantic song, more so than the comical songs in the rest of the show. I just think it would stick out like a sore thumb in the play. Hopefully, I can use it for something else some day.

Norma: Well, I guess you know best, Will, and we have plenty of other music, but it's just such a heart-wrenching melody.

Will: Yes, heart-wrenching does describe it. That's why I want the lyrics to be just right for it, and sometimes these things can't be rushed.

[Voices are heard offstage as if people are entering the house.]

Will: That must be Eldred and Ernie. I hope you're right that Lord Breakus is the right role for Ernie.

Norma: Oh, I think he's a fine actor. He's matured a lot these last few years, and he did tour with an acting company for a while.

[Eldred (Colonel Foster) and Ernie (Lord Breakus) enter. Ernie is a handsome young man in his late twenties, as suiting a male lead. Eldred is middle-aged. After some ad-libbed greetings, they get down to business.]

Norma: Here are copies of the scripts, gentlemen.

[She hands the scripts to them and keeps one for herself. Will has everything memorized.]

Will: Now, I wanted to go over the big scene in the second act. [Everyone turns to the correct page]. This is the scene where Lord Breakus tries to get Miss D.Q. Pons to love him, even though he's only English and she wants an Englishman who is also a military man, which is why she's having such a hard time choosing between Lord Breakus and the Colonel. Eldred, put on that hat there so you look like a colonel, and Ernie, you put on that silly Napoleon hat so you look like a general.

[Eldred and Ernie put on their hats.]

Will: Now, Eldred take Miss D.Q. Pons' arm. Ernie, you stand over there as if waiting for them, and now the Colonel and Miss D.Q. Pons' enter. Begin.

[Eldred takes Norma's arm and they enact their roles.]

Colonel Foster: (with a Southern accent) I can't think of anything finer than an evening stroll by moonlight. But wait until you see the Georgia moon at my plantation. It will make your cheeks even more beautiful than they already are.

Miss D.Q. Pons: Oh, Colonel, you're such a...flirt. [Her voice drops with the last word as she catches sight of Lord Breakus, although she doesn't recognize him in the dark.]

Colonel: A Southern gentleman is nothing but sincere.

[Miss D.Q. Pons ignores Colonel Foster and shakes off his arm before speaking to Lord Breakus.]

Miss D.Q. Pons: Sir, are you a major general?

Lord Breakus: I am.

Miss D.Q. Pons: (excited at hearing his accent) Oh, and you're English, too!

Lord Breakus: I am.

Miss D.Q. Pons: Would you happen to be looking for a wife?

Lord Breakus: I am.

Miss D.Q. Pons: You know, I have never kissed a man. I have promised I will only kiss the man I will wed, and that man can only be an English military man, and then I will never kiss any other man.

Lord Breakus: Would you like to kiss me?

Will: Eldred, exit stage right.

[Eldred steps backwards and sits on the sofa.]

Miss D.Q. Pons: (trying to decide whether to kiss Lord Breakus) Perhaps first we could go inside my cottage where the light is better. Something seems familiar about you, and I don't want to kiss you until I'm sure I want you. After all, the kiss will seal the deal so it can't be given hastily. You do look familiar. Haven't I met you before?

Lord Breakus: Let's stay outdoors. I've always heard that kisses in the dark are much nicer.

Miss D.Q. Pons: Well, just step into the moonlight then so I can see you better.

Lord Breakus: Oh no, I couldn't possibly, for I've always understood darkness was best for kissing, my dear.

[Lord Breakus sings "Mister Moon-Man Turn Off The Light." As he sings, he persuades her to kiss him before she can recognize him and realize he's only pretending to be a military man. The Colonel, too old and tired to participate in such a sprightly song, has resigned himself to sitting and looking on in dejection as they sing.]

Lord Breakus:

When the Moon is shining yellow
And a girlie with her fellow
Both are getting nice and mellow
In the bright moonlight.

Miss D.Q. Pons:

Then the light-man will discover
Sweethearts keeping under cover
Soon he hears that girl and lover
Say to him, "Put out that light."

Both:
Turn off your light, Mr. Moon-Man
Go and hide your face behind a cloud;
Can't you see that we want to spoon, Man,
Two is company and three's a crowd.

Lord Breakus:

I'll take my lady to a shady place where I can hug my baby

Miss D.Q. Pons:

And we'll say to you, "Good-night, Good-night."

Both:

We want to tease and squeeze,
if you please,
Mister Moon-Man turn off the light.

Lord Breakus:

All you lads and little misses,
Like to have your hugs and kisses,
But remember half the bliss is
When it's dark as it can be.

Miss D.Q. Pons:
If once more I start my pleading,
Tell him darkness we are needing,
In case my pleading he is heeding,
You must do the same as we.

Together:

Turn off your light, Mr. Moon-Man
Go and hide your face behind a cloud;
Can't you see that we want to spoon, Man,
Two is company and three's a crowd.

Mister Moon-Man turn off the light.

Lord Breakus:

I'll take my lady to a shady place where I can hug my baby

Miss D.Q. Pons:

And we'll say to you, "Good-night, Good-night."

Both:

We want to tease and squeeze,
if you please,
Mister Moon-Man turn off the light.

Mister Moon-Man turn off the light.

[At the song's end, Lord Breakus begins to kiss Miss D.Q. Pons passionately. Will, frowning, breaks it up.]

Will: That's enough. That's enough! [He looks jealous but is trying to restrain his temper.] That's enough rehearsing for today. I'm feeling kind of tired.

Ernie: I'm not sure that scene went so well. Don't you think we should rehearse it again?

[Ernie moves in for another kiss with Norma.]

Will: (glaring at him) Not today.

Norma: But, Will, we only have a few weeks until the play premieres.

Will: We have time. Now I want you all to go home and think positive thoughts about what a success this show is going to be.

[They all prepare to leave.]

Will: Norma, hold on a minute. I want to go over something in the script with you.

[The boys depart.]

Will: Norma, I don't think Ernie is a very good actor.

Norma: Oh, Will.

Will: Seriously, why don't we replace him with Clarence Brown? Now that boy can sing.

Norma: You're just getting nervous about the show, Will. Ernie will do just fine. Now I have to get going, too.

[Norma exits.]

Will: I'm afraid Ernie will do too fine.

Scene 3: The Adams House, July 1905

[The screen changes, showing headlines proclaiming the popularity of the show as "Mister Moon-Man Turn Off The Light" is played in the background.]

New Opera Scores a Hit—Miss D.Q. Pons Greeted by a Bumper Crowd at Marquette Opera House

Norma Ross Receives Standing Ovation for Her Role as Miss D.Q. Pons

Ishpeming Exuberantly Embraces Miss D.Q. Pons

Will Adams Off to Hancock for Performance of Miss D.Q. Pons

Calumet Theatre Sells Out for Operetta by Local Composer and Lyricist

Sault Ste. Marie All Locked Up with Love for Miss D.Q. Pons

Success of Miss D.Q. Pons Results in Encore Performance in Marquette

[Will is lying in his bed with Norma beside him. They have just returned from the success of *Miss D. Q. Pons'* performance. Norma is still in her costume.]

Norma: (tucking him into bed) There, are you comfortable now? It's been such a long day that I'm sure you'll sleep well tonight.

Will: Sleep? You know I rarely sleep. I don't think I'll ever sleep again after tonight. Did you hear how they applauded?

Norma: (smiling) Yes, Will, but don't forget some of that applause was for me.

Will: Oh, yes, of course. They loved you, Norma. How could they not? But did you see how they rushed the stage when I didn't come out? I never experienced anything so thrilling in my life.

[Mr. and Mrs. Adams and Bertha enter.]

Mr. and Mrs. Adams and Bertha in unison: Author! Author!

Mrs. Adams: What a wonderful performance!

Bertha: Oh, I wish the Doctor could have come home from California with me, but I'm so glad to have seen your play, Will.

Mr. Adams: Play—you call that a play? Why, it was a masterpiece!

Mrs. Adams: And, Norma, you were marvelous.

Will: I told you I'd make you a star someday, Norma.

Norma: (smiling) Yes, Will, you did.

Bertha: Oh, Norma, how exciting it must have been for you, and to get to play opposite such a handsome male lead as Ernie Ludlow. I would have said "Yes" to him myself after he sung that Mr. Moon-Man song, only I have the Doctor, of course, but nothing would stop you from—

Will: (interrupting) That's enough, Bertha. I thought Ernie was rather flat myself, and in the second act, he was late for his cue.

Norma: Stop it, Will. He did fine.

Mrs. Adams: Well, we all better get to bed now. It's been a long day.

[Everyone exits except Norma, who stays back a moment, then turns to Will.]

Norma: Thank you, Will.

[She turns to exit, but Will calls her back.]

Will: Norma, did you really think the show was good?

Norma: (turning again to face him) Oh, Will, this has been the best night of my life. It was wonderful and you made it happen.

Will: (with love in his eyes) I couldn't have done it without my Miss D.Q. Pons. I'm so glad she didn't marry Lord Breakus for real.

Norma: No fear of that.

The Marquette Opera House where *Miss D.Q. Pons* premiered. Built in 1892 by city benefactors J.M. Longyear and Peter White, the opera house could seat 900. It hosted many national celebrities including Lillian Russell, Lon Chaney, John Philip Sousa, and W.C. Fields. It would tragically burn down during the great blizzard of January 1938.

Will Adams personally attended all of the rehearsals of *Miss D.Q. Pons*, being borne on his patented bed back and forth to the theatre. On the opening night of the play, his bed was placed on an elevation in the theatre wings so he could view the production. Following the performance, when the audience shouted "Author!" he could not make an appearance so the audience swarmed upon the stage to congratulate him.

Scene 4: The Adams House, Early August 1909

[Bertha is beside Will's bed.]

Will: I'm glad you're home visiting, Bertha. I just wish you would stay longer.

Bertha: I'm glad too, but you know how the Doctor loves to travel, and he doesn't like to be here except in the summer. The winters are just too tough.

Will: I know. But since Father died, I think all Mother has to live for are your visits home.

Bertha: She has you too, Will. She's written to me many times that she doesn't know what she would do if she didn't have you to cheer her.

Will: She keeps up a good front, but—

[Mrs. Adams enters.]

Mrs. Adams: Will, you have a guest. It's....

[Lillian Russell, age forty-eight, enters while Mrs. Adams remains too star-struck to finish her sentence. The famous actress pauses in all her glamour to give the full effect of her charismatic presence.]

Will: (squinting since he is going blind, but trying to hide the fact) Norma, is that you? You put on weight.

Lillian: (laughs as she walks toward him) Don't you like my famous hourglass figure?

Will: Who is it? I'm sorry. The light is in my eyes.

Bertha: (looking at him strangely as if he must be blind not to recognize their famous guest) Will, it's Lillian Russell, the famous actress. I told you she was in town. I...oh, I'm so pleased to meet you, Miss Russell.

Lillian: It's my pleasure, my dear.

Bertha: I'm Mrs. Dawson, Will's sister, and of course, this is my brother.

Will: Lillian Russell? A pleasure, ma'am, but what are you "russelling" around these parts for?

Lillian: (laughing) You have such a fine opera house in Marquette that I had to come to perform here. Mr. Adams, won't you be coming to see me in my new play, *Wildfire*?

Will: I'm afraid I'm not able to get out much anymore.

Lillian: Yes, so I understand, which is why I've come to visit you. I met your charming friend, Miss Ross, last night after my performance. She told me she wanted to remember every minute of it so she could tell it all to her dear friend, Mr. Adams. She told me all about you, and when I heard you had composed your own comic operetta without being able to move a muscle, I had to come see you for myself.

Bertha: Oh, bless Norma.

Will: (grinning mischievously) I'm highly honored, Miss Russell. I've been telling Norma for years that the only woman on the stage she could take lessons from in beauty, poise, and talent is yourself.

Lillian: (laughs) Thank you. You're very kind.

[Norma enters. She gratefully smiles at Miss Russell, then goes to Will and clasps his hand.]

Norma: I see you found out my surprise, Will.

Will: I can't think of a nicer one.

Mrs. Adams: Oh, Norma, we're just absolutely thrilled. Thank you.

Lillian: Norma wanted me to come and sing for you, but I'm afraid I've had so much trouble with my voice that I don't sing anymore. I've switched to dramatic roles, you understand.

Mrs. Adams: That's all right, Miss Russell. It's a pleasure just to have you as a guest in our home. I wish my husband could have lived to see you.

Bertha: (patting Mrs. Adams shoulder) And it's too bad my husband, the Doctor, is out. I know he'll be sorry he missed you.

Norma: Will, I told Miss Russell all about our operetta. That's why she insisted on meeting you.

Lillian: Yes, I think it's amazing what you've accomplished.

Will: No different than you, Miss Russell. Just because you can't sing anymore is no reason for you to stop being on stage. We have to do what we can to keep this world bright.

Lillian: I couldn't agree more, and I'd love to hear some of your brightness if Miss Ross will indulge me by singing some of your operetta.

Norma: Oh, I'd be too embarrassed to sing before a professional like you.

Lillian: Nonsense, my dear. Please do.

Norma: But I don't have the score for the operetta here. It's at my house.

Will: That's no problem, Norma. You can sing the piece I just finished.

Norma: What piece?

Will: That love song I always promised you I'd finish. The Doctor wrote down the lyrics for me this morning.

Bertha: Yes, it's sitting on the piano, Norma.

Norma: Oh, Will. What a wonderful surprise.

Will: There's two copies of it. Bertha, would you play the piano so Norma can just sing?

[Bertha goes to the piano and gives Norma a copy of the music so she can read the lyrics.]

Lillian: What's it called?

Norma: (feeling uncomfortable as she reads the title) "You Will Not Love Me."

[Bertha begins to play. As Norma sings, she keeps looking at Will, realizing he wrote the song specifically for her.]

Norma:

> You will not love me; you won't say why.
> Your face shows love, but your lips deny.
> You say you're ill, you won't last long.
> But love's a pill that can cure all wrong.

> I should go off; find some other beau
> But he'd be just another old Joe.
> I love you only; I cannot lie.
> You will not love me; you won't say why.

> You say you might die; well, so might I.
> You will not love me; you won't say why.
> Would my love be truly so bad
> That being dead would make you glad?

> I'll make you coffee, lay out your pills.
> Checking your pulse will give me thrills.
> Why can't you see where my heart does lead?
> I want to care for your every need.

[When Norma finishes singing, everyone applauds.]

Mrs. Adams: That was beautiful.

Bertha: And funny, too.

Lillian: (clasping her hands together) I think it was just splendid. I wish I could sing it myself.

Norma: You're very kind, Miss Russell, but it's nothing compared to what you can do.

Will: Nevertheless, Miss Russell, Norma is my inspiration.

Lillian: Yes, I can see that.

[Norma blushes. Mrs. Adams and Bertha exchange glances and raised eyebrows. An awkward moment of silence is broken by Miss Russell.]

Lillian: So, Mr. Adams, will you be writing another operetta?

Will: No, I don't think so. I feel that once you achieve success in one thing, you might as well move on to something else. There are so many things to accomplish in this life, and I'm afraid because of my ossification, I only have limited time.

Lillian: I think you have more energy than any young man I know, and far more genius if you can write music and lyrics like what I just heard.

Will: Thank you. One can't let life's obstacles stand in the way of one's success.

Lillian: (laughing) I am so impressed by you, Mr. Adams, not just for your humor but for your spirit. Someone should write a book about you.

Will: That would be wonderful so long as the author doesn't say I'm a cripple or bedridden. I'm not so badly off, you know. Had it been otherwise, I might have become the subject of a trust investigating committee or a bank president. But I'd rather be literary than sordid any day.

Lillian: With your wit and literary talent, I don't see how anyone could think there was anything wrong with you.

Will: Yes, but every specimen of my writing is a silent story of how this author saved himself from cerrebrius combustion. Genius burns, and if I don't release it, I am certain I would explode. As it is, my body has grown stiff as wood, so I suspect I am highly flammable.

Lillian: (smiling) I certainly hope not. I think the world is much enriched by your humor.

[Will nods in acknowledgment.]

Lillian: Well, I must be going. I have a rehearsal to attend this afternoon.

Mrs. Adams: (quickly standing) Thank you so much for coming, Miss Russell. It's been such an honor.

Lillian: Oh, no, the honor was all mine.

Norma: Thank you, Miss Russell.

Will: (slyly) It has been a pleasure, but now the hourglass must be turned or it will run dry.

[Lillian, laughing, poses to show off her hourglass figure for him.]

Mrs. Adams: Allow me to show you out, Miss Russell.

[Mrs. Adams and Bertha exit with Miss Russell.]

Norma: Will, wasn't she wonderful?

Will: The second most wonderful woman I've ever met.

[Norma, feeling awkward, sits down at the piano and quietly plays a verse of "You Will Not Love Me." After a minute, she turns around.]

Norma: Thank you for finishing the song, Will.

Will: Do you like it?

Norma: Ye-es. I think it's lovely...a bit heartbreaking, but with comic relief.... Bittersweet, really. [She looks sad, as if holding back words.]

Will: (after a moment, then awkwardly as if changing the subject) Well, I'm glad you like it. So I believe tomorrow is the day you're leaving to visit Grace in Detroit.

Norma: Yes, I really should be going now. I still have to pack. [She gets up to leave.]

Will: Who'd have ever thought that pesky little sister of yours would become a nurse.

Norma: (smiling) I think we were all surprised.

Will: Say hello to her for me.

Norma: I will, but Will....

[He looks at her, waiting, afraid of what she'll say.]

Norma: Will, it's a beautiful song, and I appreciate you finishing it. But it feels...well, sort of...personal in a way—

Will: It's just a song, Norma. I mean, yes, I wrote it special for you, but it's just a song.

Norma: No, I don't think it is. Will, I know you're not in the best of health, but—

Will: You're quite observant, aren't you?

Norma: No, be serious for a moment. I mean, I know you can't, uh...but I hope you do know that it doesn't matter to me...I mean—

Will: Oh, don't start that, Norma. It's just a song.

Norma: But, Will. I don't want you to think I'm unhappy. It's enough for me—

Will: You better get home to pack. You don't want to miss your train and disappoint all those eligible young bachelors in Detroit who are just waiting to catch a glimpse of the Belle of Marquette.

Norma: Will, will you just let me finish what I'm—

Will: I know what you're going to say, but you're not listening to me. Norma, it's about time you find a husband.

Norma: I don't see why I should go find a husband just for the sake of having one.

Will: I don't want you to spend your life alone, Norma. You deserve better than that.

Norma: You're alone.

Will: I'm a man. It's different for a man. I have my work.

Norma: So do I, Will. You know I'm married to my work—to teaching and my music.

Will: But wouldn't you like a family someday?

Norma: I have hundreds of students. They're my children, and just think how many lives I can touch by instilling a love of music in them.

Will: You deserve more, Norma. Look for it before it's too late.

Norma: Maybe I don't want to look for it.

Will: Then you're a fool. You can't expect anything big or great to happen for you by just sitting around here all day.

Norma: Just sitting around here? You let me tell you something, Mr. Will Adams—

[Mrs. Adams enters]

Mrs. Adams: Whatever is wrong? What's all the shouting about? Are you ill, Will?

Will: No, Mother. Norma and I were just enacting a scene from a play.

Mrs. Adams: Oh, what's the play?

Norma: *Love's Labour's Lost.*

[Mrs. Adams looks confused. Will looks away from Norma, afraid of what she might say in front of his mother.]

Norma: I better be going. Thank you, Mrs. Adams, for your hospitality. [Norma turns to leave.]

Will: Norma—

Norma: (with her back to him) Yes.

[He doesn't say anything. Norma hesitates. After a moment, to break the silence, Mrs. Adams speaks.]

Mrs. Adams: Have a nice trip, Norma.

[Norma nods and rushes out.]

Autographed photo that Lillian Russell gave to Will Adams. It was later donated by Norma Ross to the
Marquette Regional History Center.

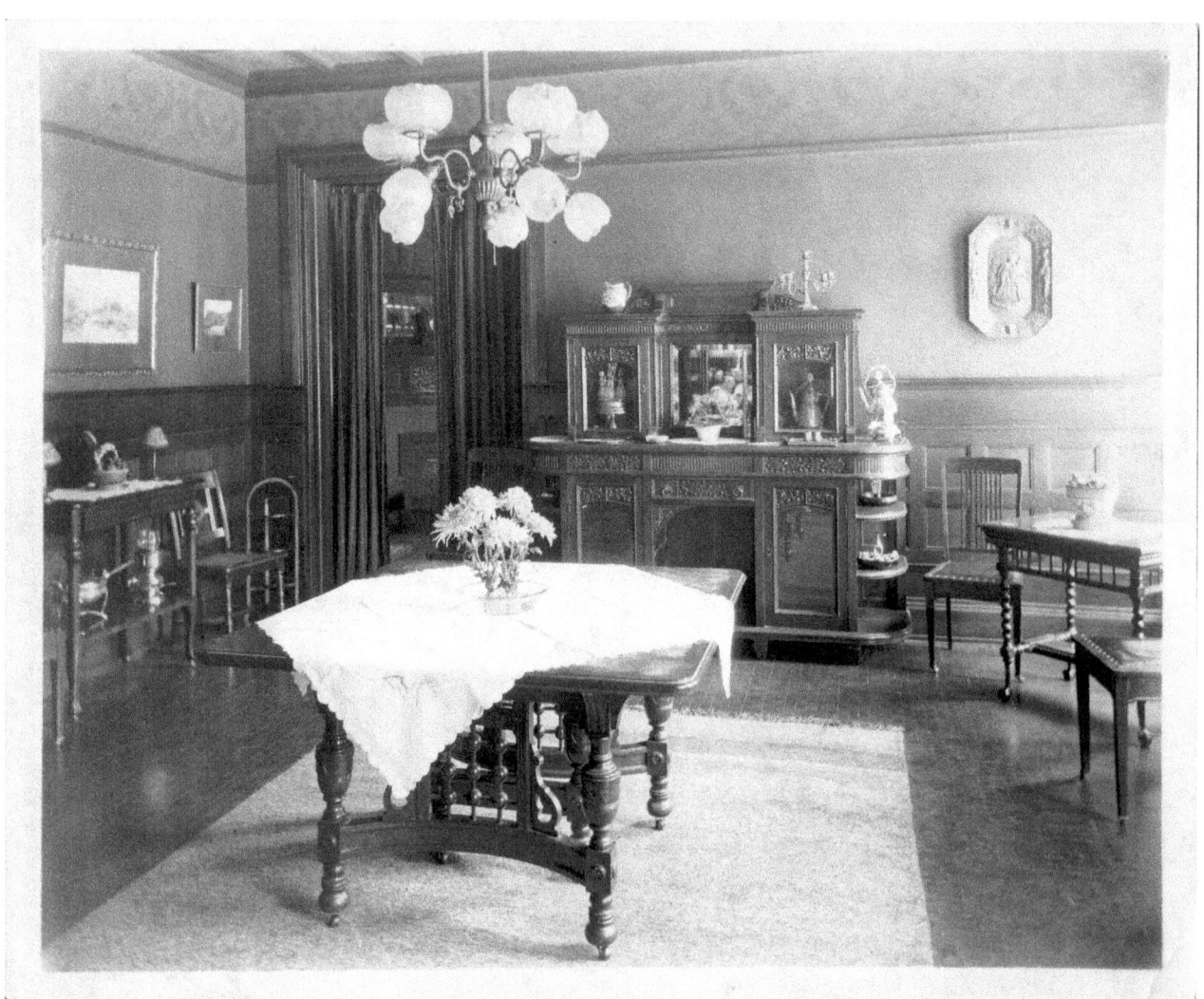

Interior of Grace's House. The interior was actually that of the Marquette Matthews' House on Blaker and Bluff Streets.

Scene 5: Grace's House in Detroit, August 10, 1909

[Grace and Norma are sitting at the table finishing supper. Norma is listlessly moving around her fork on her plate and staring, looking depressed.]

Grace: Norma, I'm glad you came, but I wish you weren't so glum.

Norma: I know. I just can't stop thinking about the argument I had with Will. Why did he have to spoil everything by writing those lyrics to that beautiful song the way he did? I wish—I just wish he would let me love him. It wouldn't hurt him any.

Grace: Why don't you tell him that?

Norma: I tried, but...oh, it's no use. He's as stubborn as a tree and won't let me broach the subject whenever I do try.

Grace: What would you say to him if he were here now? Tell me. Imagine you're talking to him. That might help you express yourself better when you see him next time.

[Norma hesitates.]

Grace: Don't be shy. I'll play devil's advocate and reply as if I were him. Go ahead.

[Reprise of "You Will Not Love Me"]

> **Norma:**
>
> You will not love me; you won't say why.
> Your face shows love, but your lips deny.
> You say you're ill, you won't last long,
> But love's a pill that can cure all wrong.
>
> I should go off, find some other beau
> But he'd be just another old Joe.
> I love you only; I cannot lie.
> You will not love me; you won't say why.
>
> **Grace:** (responding as Will)
> Though my life will not be long
> That does not mean that our love is wrong.
> My will is strong, but for how long?
> How can I know just what feelings belong?

Tell me how long that I must deny—
What my heart feels. I will not cry.
I care for you only—I don't want to lie.
You should not love me—and you know why.

Norma: Oh, it's no use, Grace. I better go to bed. I'll need my rest if you're taking me to see all the sights in Detroit tomorrow, and I want to write a quick note to Father so he knows I got here safely before I go to sleep.

Grace: All right. I think I'll go to bed early, too.

[Grace exits. Norma retrieves some paper and a pen and sits down to write her letter. For a moment, she pauses, as if debating whether to write to Will. Then she becomes decisive.]

Norma: Father can wait. I just can't stand leaving Will on bad terms, and I did say I would write to him, but....

[She picks up the pen and begins writing. Voiceover begins.]

Dear Will,

I've safely arrived in Detroit. I am sorry we had an argument before I left. I would never wish to upset you, but I need you to understand why I have made the choice I have for my life. I said that my music and teaching were enough for me, and that's true. At least it has to be true because I can't have the only man I've ever wanted, and no one else could take his place for me. You know you are that man, Will....

[The scene fades as she continues to write.]

Norma Ross, possibly in her *Miss D.Q. Pons* costume

Scene 6: The Adams House, August 10, 1909

[Will is dictating to his mother, who is busy writing.]

Mrs. Adams: What are you planning to title this new book, Will?

Will: *Old Saws with New Teeth.*

Mrs. Adams: That's an odd name.

Will: On the contrary, I find its humor quite biting.

Mrs. Adams: I'm afraid I don't get it.

Will: Well, it's a metaphor for how I've become like a wooden man, being so stiff and all. You know that Wooden Man that Mr. Harlow built in his backyard. I like to think we have some things in common.

Mrs. Adams: (laughing) Like what?

Will: Well, we both come from illustrious ancestry.

Mrs. Adams: And how is that?

Will: For beginners, the Wooden Man was created by Marquette's first mayor, Amos Harlow, so you might say Mr. Harlow adopted him. And you and Father adopted me, and both Father and Mr. Harlow have been mayors of Marquette. And the greatest similarity is that both of our bodies are wooden.

Mrs. Adams: I see.

Will: Now read back that last part you just wrote down for me, will you, Mother?

Mrs. Adams: (reading from a sheet of paper) Hello, Folks. The name's Mr. Wood, plain Wood. If there were anything Mahoganish about me, I'd buy a ticket for bad Axe and have it cut out.

Will: Good. Good.

Mrs. Adams: (setting down pen and paper) I don't know how you can continue to be so imaginative, Will.

Will: The genius burns, Mother. I have no choice. I'm blessed with energy despite my ailment.

Mrs. Adam: I know. You keep telling me that. Your energy and spirit are what have kept me going these last few years since your father died. He would be so proud of you for being the man of the house now that he's gone.

Will: I wish I could do more to make it a home for you, Mother. Sometimes, I wonder that you don't think of marrying again.

Mrs. Adams: Oh, I couldn't marry again.

Will: Why not? Bertha did. And it's been nearly three years now since Father died.

Mrs. Adams: (laughing) Bertha was a lot younger than me when she remarried, and while I know she loved George, she wasn't married to him but seventeen months. That's nowhere near all the years your father and I were married.

Will: I know. But the day is coming when I'll be gone, and I don't want you to be lonely.

Mrs. Adams: I think there's another young lady you're worried about seeing lonely.

Will: Norma spends too much time with me. It's not good for her. She deserves more.

Mrs. Adams: You had an argument with her before she left, didn't you?

Will: Not an argument. At least...let's just say I made myself clear. I know she thinks she can be noble by keeping the flame burning for me, but it's not right. It's for her own good.

Mrs. Adams: I think you're the one being noble, Will.

Will: You know I'm right, Mother. I'm grateful for her friendship, though. And I'm grateful to you and Father for adopting me. Imagine what my life might have been like otherwise with this condition.

Mrs. Adams: We've all benefited just as much from having you in our lives, Will. Look at Bertha; she might never have married the Doctor without your help.

Will: That's true. I've tried to make the world brighter for people however I could.

Mrs. Adams: Your cantankerous sense of humor has certainly done that, Will.

Will: Cantankerous, hey? Sounds like a form of tree cancer, which is just about what I have, seeing as how I'm like a piece of petrified wood now.

Mrs. Adams: (shaking her head) You and your wood metaphors. Well, I better go see about supper. Do you want to eat out on the porch? I'll bring us each a tray and sit with you if you like.

Will: Sure, Mother.

[Mrs. Adams exits as Will continues talking to himself.]

Will: Yes, I'm like wood in more ways than one. Kind of like Mr. Harlow's Wooden Man. I just can't help identifying with him. I mean, he's a tree made to resemble a human, and I'm a human who resembles a tree. If you searched back far enough, you'd probably find we were branches from the same family tree. If only Mr. Wood could talk, perhaps we could untangle our mutual roots.

[Will closes his eyes for a moment. A lighting effect is used to suggest something mystical is happening, as if a light from heaven is shining down upon him. He rises stiffly from his bed as if his spirit is leaving his body. He takes difficult wood-like steps, puts on a hat, and uses a walking stick to add to his Wooden Man appearance. Then he walks to center stage as a spotlight shines on him. He speaks to the audience as Mr. Wood with the tone and composure of a stand-up comedian.]

Mr. Wood: Hello, Folks. The name's Mr. Wood, plain Wood. If there were anything Mahoganish about me, I'd buy a ticket for bad Axe and have it cut out.

Now, I understand some of you are curious about my family's roots. They go way back in history. It was the Wood family that kept the ark afloat. I'll leave it to Noah if we didn't. He woodn't lie about it if he could, which he can't. I received a telegram last week from his wife, reading as follows: "He is Dead-Wood."

It was the Woods who built up America. Even today you will hear the cultured and refined connoisseur of antiques speak of the beautiful woodwork of the seventeenth century. No home was complete without a woodhouse. It was a necessity, a crying need, for which the family put up a howl—even the Dogwood bark for it.

During the presidential campaign of 1824, my father was invited to take the Stump for "Old Hickory," but he was unable to leave at the time. Father's only shortcoming during life was the Sap habit, which he accumulated hoping to rid himself of rheumatism in his limbs. It led to Wood alcohol, and eventually Woodlawn cemetery.

Mother was a Knott from Pine Ridge, and was Sycamore or less. She was uncomplaining, however, and never said to Father, "This is Hard, Wood"; not mother; she didn't wish to introduce a Weeping Willow into the house.

There were two other boys in our family. The elder, Hew Wood, met his death in the village sawmill rehearsing a Dialogue to be given for the benefit of the Ancient Order of United Woodmen. My other brother was of nomadic tendencies; in other words, a Hobo—so we called him Drift Wood. Some day he may wash ashore.

The sweetest member of our family was my sister, Rose Wood. Unfortunately, she was married to a man named Slippery Elm. Slippery was too smooth to pay her board, so she starved to death at Oak Park.

As for myself, I am the proprietor of a beautiful Block house at Shingleton, surrounded by a magnificent Lumber Yard. You should see the Tuberfours I raised last season.

If my remarks have had a slight chestnut flavor, it is because I have the chestnut blight; in fact, I'm about ready to rot and not long for this world.

Nevertheless, I hope we may meet again someday where the Woodbine twineth.

I am, Yours to an Oak Finish,

Mr. WOOD

[Mr. Wood awkwardly attempts to bow as the curtain closes.]

Harlow's Wooden Man

Will's book *Old Saws with New Teeth*

Scene 7: Grace's House in Detroit, August 11, 1909

[The curtain opens to Norma and Grace seated at a table having breakfast.]

Grace: Norma, I can't believe how quickly your visit is passing by. It's been so fun having you here, but I imagine you're anxious to get home.

Norma: Oh, no, Grace. I'm enjoying myself so much.

Grace: Don't lie to me, Norma. I know you're happy to see me, but I suspect you have someone at home who is always on your mind.

[Norma is silent. She pretends to be busy drinking her coffee as Grace stares at her.]

Grace: Norma, I don't like to see you breaking your heart. You know it's not good for you.

Norma: I can't help it, Grace.

Grace: Will wouldn't want you to go on waiting for something he can never give you.

[Norma focuses on buttering her toast without answering.]

Grace: Norma, please listen to—

[Grace is interrupted by a knock at the door. She sighs and gets up to open it. She is surprised to see a telegram boy.]

Telegram Boy: Telegram, ma'am.

Grace: Thank you. [She gives him a tip and takes the telegram from him. She closes the door after him and looks at the telegram.] Norma, it's addressed to you. It's from Father.

[Norma takes it from her and reads it out loud.]

Norma: August 10, 1909. Stop. Norma. Stop. Come home. Stop. Will died tonight from heart failure. Stop. Funeral on Friday. Stop. Father.

[Norma breaks into tears.]

Scene 8: St. Paul's Episcopal Church, Friday, August 13, 1909

[A choir is in the background behind the pulpit. Mourners are assembled on both sides of the stage. Mrs. Adams stands by the edge of the stage, greeting the mourners. Norma enters accompanied by Grace.]

Mrs. Adams: (hugging her) Norma, I'm so glad you made it home in time.

Norma: I am, too. I think I'm still in shock. I didn't expect it.

Mrs. Adams: None of us did. It was very sudden.

[Rev. Bates Burt moves to the pulpit and clears his throat as a sign that it's time to begin.]

Mrs. Adams: We'll talk later, dear, but I brought you this letter you sent. It came the day after Will died. I didn't feel right opening it.

Norma: (sadly taking the envelope) Thank you.

[Norma and Mrs. Adams take their seats as the pallbearers enter, carrying a casket, which is set center stage in front of the pulpit. Mourners are wiping their tears as the pallbearers take their seats.]

Rev. Bates Burt: Dearly beloved, we are gathered here today to pay our final respects to our dear friend and brother in Christ, Will S. Adams. For years, we watched him bravely live with a medical condition no doctor was able to explain. Many of you remember him as a young boy when he first came to Marquette, adopted by his loving parents, Sidney and Harriet Adams. We all loved to listen to him sing in the boys' choir here at St. Paul's. We were all amazed by his quick wit and his tremendous memory, his literary genius, and most of all, his *willpower* to make the most of every moment he had. At an early age, he knew his life would be cut short, and now he has left us at the young age of thirty-one. But there are few men I know who can say they did so much with their lives, much less in such a short time, or who brought so much happiness and inspiration to others.

Will told me once that he compared his condition to that the Apostle Paul wrote about in Corinthians—the thorn in the flesh, and he believed the Good Lord gave it to him for the very reason Paul cites: because otherwise he'd have been too brilliant and great, and so God had to remind him who was the real power in this world. For all Will's wit and literary success, the greatest legacy I think he left us was his example of patience and how he made the most out of what God left him. He truly multiplied his talents and gave of them generously. I know I am better for having known Will, and many of you have told me you feel the same.

Few outside his family knew Will better than his good friend, Miss Ross. I know she needs no introduction to you. I've asked her to say a few words. Norma, would you come forward?

[Norma walks up to the pulpit.]

Norma: Thank you, Reverend. There are no words I can say to express how talented Will was or how much we'll miss him. But I do know he loved music and he would want us always to keep our spirits up, so I've asked Reverend Burt for permission to sing with the choir a favorite song of Will's that I think reflects his spirit. Most of you know the song so I invite you all to join me.

Norma:

My life flows on in endless song;
Above earth's lamentation.
I hear the real though far-off hymn
That hails a new creation.

All:

No storm can shake my inmost calm,
While to that rock I'm clinging.
Since Love is Lord of heaven and earth,
How can I keep from singing?

Through all the tumult and the strife,
I hear that music ringing;
It sounds and echoes in my soul;
How can I keep from singing?

No storm can shake my inmost calm,
While to that rock I'm clinging.
Since Love is Lord of heaven and earth,
How can I keep from singing?

What though the tempest 'round me roar,
I hear the truth it liveth.
What though the darkness 'round me close,
Songs in the night it giveth.

No storm can shake my inmost calm,
While to that rock I'm clinging.
Since Love is Lord of heaven and earth,
How can I keep from singing?

Excerpt from the opening of the *Detroit Free Press* article describing Will and Norma's collaboration on *Miss D.Q. Pons*.

Marquette's Ossified Man

Sunday, March 18, 1906

C. Nick Stark

From an upstairs apartment of a Marquette flat echoed the strains of a joyous melody. The listing air of a comic opera was borne to the nearby streets of the snow-shrouded Michigan city that is so rich in romance and historical interest. A woman's voice, clear, strong and sweet, blended with a man's tenor. Together the vocal intonations rose above the moan of the winter tempest that raged outside, dispelling gloom as the dawning of a bright day dissipates the shadows of night.

The picture revealed in that apartment was one of remarkable contrasts. Seated at a piano was a young woman, attractive not only in face; her soul was in the music she produced.

One could close one's eyes to the surroundings and imagine one was seated in a theater listening to some comic divinity.

A few paces from the piano, upon a patented couch made expressly for his use, lay the owner of the tenor voice. He, too, was inspired by the happy quality of the song. His face, strong in outline and betraying unmistakable traces of comeliness, wore a joyous expression. His soul also was in the song.

Scene 9: Norma's Apartment, 1963

[Fred and Norma are looking through a trunk. Norma is seated as Fred pulls out items, handing them to her.]

Norma: I'm sorry I didn't have anything else to interest you, Fred.

Fred: (pulling out an envelope) That's okay. This is the last of it. Looks like a letter that was never opened.

Norma: (reaching for it and looking at it with a bit of surprise) Oh, yes. That wouldn't interest you, I'm sure. [She tucks it in her pocket.]

Fred: (picking up some papers) You don't mind my borrowing these other papers, though?

Norma: No, go ahead. I hope they're helpful.

Fred: Okay. Well, I better be going. Thanks for everything you shared with me, Norma. Don't bother getting up. I can see myself out.

[Norma turns in her chair to follow him with her eyes as he goes to the door.]

Norma: Goodbye, Fred. If I come across anything else that I think might interest you, I'll let you know.

Fred: Thank you. I'd appreciate that. Goodbye.

[Fred exits. Norma is silent for a moment. Then she pulls out the envelope, opens it, and reads it out loud.]

Norma: I have known my great love and that's more than a million women ever know who marry without love.... I just want you to be clear how much I do love you and why it is impossible, therefore, for me to consider marriage to someone else....

[Norma lowers the letter. As she speaks, the song "You Will Not Love Me" softly begins in the background.]

Norma: You never even got to read it, Will, but I know you knew. I know you knew how I loved you, and I know you would have been proud of all the children I've taught, all the plays and concerts and musical events I've helped with. I've kept our dreams alive for all these years, Will, even though it seems like just yesterday when we met. It was grand while it lasted, Will.

[She clutches the letter to her heart as tears run down her face.]

CURTAIN

Experience the Power of *Willpower*

by Director Moire Embley

Director Moire Embley

A sunny mid-August day in Marquette, Michigan. An operatic aria fills the air from a west side apartment. The melody is from an original composition, "You Will Not Love Me" for the upcoming Marquette Regional History Center's new production *Willpower* by Tyler Tichelaar. The beautiful soprano voice of Sara Parks floats effortlessly to the piano accompaniment of composer, Jeff Bruning. As Sara soulfully sings the repeated lyric "You will not love me; you won't say why," her character, Miss Norma Ross, comes to life.

I have assisted and directed several plays in Marquette over the last fourteen years, but *Willpower* is the first original play I have had the opportunity to be a part of. In September 2013, the Marquette Regional History Center's Director, Kaye Hiebel, was scouting for a director and I was lucky to be recommended by a good friend and mentor of mine. I came into the first meeting feeling slightly shy and a bit overwhelmed to be offered such a break as a director.

I sat quietly in the large conference room surrounded by high-powered ladies, taking in the conversations, stories, and ideas that saturated the room. The focus was on a young man from Marquette in the late 1800s by the name of Will Adams. Will, I came to understand, was not your typical boy. Adopted as a young child by former Marquette Mayor Sidney and wife Harriet Adams in the early 1880s, he grew up at 200 East Ridge, the beautiful sandstone house that is now known as the "Terrace Apartments." As a youngster, Will sang in a boy's choir at St. Paul's Episcopal Church and was a noted athlete, artist, and literary mastermind by the community. After suffering a severe baseball injury to his knee, an ossifying disease began to develop in his legs. As he grew, so did the disease, until it consumed his body, slowly turning his soft tissues to stone before he passed away at thirty-one.

Will's story is not a sad one, but one of love, ambition, community, and courage. After leaving the meeting, I found myself eager and driven. This was a drama I needed to help tell on the historical stage of Kaufman Auditorium. Tyler Tichelaar, a well-known local novelist, was hired as the playwright. After Tyler released the first draft of *Willpower*, I spent an entire road trip reading the play and then reading it again. Tyler's use of public domain music was thoughtful and clever. His character delineations were accurate, concise, and well-researched. I could not put the script down. I became fascinated by his depiction of Will.

Will was not the only character in *Willpower* to stand out. His caring childhood friend Norma Ross also captured my imagination. Norma and Will met as young children, and a friendship was nurtured by their shared love for music, theatre, and literature. As Will's disease became more debilitating, Norma would visit him almost daily. They would pass the time singing to one another. When Will began to lose the use of his arms and was unable to hold a book, Norma became his eyes and hands, reading aloud to him.

After graduating from college with a degree in music from Northwestern University, Norma returned home to Marquette. Will, now in his late twenties, became fascinated with writing an operetta in which he enlisted the musical talents of his good friend. Norma and Will spent nearly three months preparing the lyrics and music. Will hummed the melodies as Norma played the piano, putting the music down on paper. *Miss D.Q. Pons* opened at the Marquette Opera House in the summer of 1905. The operetta's success spread quickly, eventually touring throughout Upper Michigan to Ishpeming, Sault Ste. Marie, Hancock, and Calumet.

As I read the first draft of *Willpower*, I couldn't help feeling that there was more between Will and Norma. I met with Tyler and Jessica "Red" Bays in mid-January 2014 to discuss the first draft. I hadn't met Tyler before and I was very nervous to discuss some edits I thought could be made. My approach was only to assist in using my theatre background to help guide the script to the stage. Some minimal character enhancements were made along with some plotline adaptations. Red and I left the meeting with Tyler more excited than ever. I felt he graciously considered my notes, however standing his ground on some changes. Between Red, myself, and Tyler, ideas bounced back and forth as we found our creative balance.

Tyler quickly came back with the second draft. Every note we had discussed was in the script. Tyler's attention to detail and respect for my creative vision as director was admirable. I frequently would tell him my job is to bring his story to the stage, but in a way I feel that this play is a collaborative effort between Red, Tyler, and me. With only minimal edits to be made, Tyler quickly moved on to the third draft.

After the script became finalized, I searched for the best artistic staff I could find. Suzanne Shahbazi, well known for her work with the Lake Superior Youth Theatre, agreed to do costumes. Jalina Olgren joined the production; she is one of the most talented stage managers we have in the Marquette community. Lastly, Jeff Bruning, a brilliant pianist, voice teacher, and music virtuoso, signed on. To round out the creative production team, Jessica "Red" Bays became my right hand, my support, and my promotional guru.

Casting is always a wonderful process, offering a director a first-time glimpse into seeing the characters come alive. Within the two days of auditions and one day of callbacks, I was blessed with an overwhelming amount of talent. I feel fortunate as a director to work in a community with high talent, quality vocals, and acting ability. The final casting after auditions can be sometimes difficult. It is important undoubtedly to see a specific character within an actor. A director must also see that the character, small at times, be in the actor's potential.

Although *Willpower* is a straight play, public domain music and old ragtime songs are used. This piano style popular from the nineteenth century through the early twentieth century gives the play a musical feel and also illustrates how music was an integral part of Will and Norma's relationship. There was one piece composed for the play, "You Will Not Love Me," by Jeff Bruning and lyrics by Tyler Tichelaar.

Jeff wrote the piece, which captured the feel of the romantic ballads at that time. Tyler's lyrics possess a witty touch, as if Will wrote them himself.

For the set design, historical images were used, and to find them, I did extensive research at the J.M. Longyear Research Library. Using the expertise of research librarians Rosemary Michelin and Beth Gruber, the three of us spent hours hunting for Will and Norma's past in genealogy files, photos, books, newspapers, magazines, and plat books. I have great respect and gratitude for all the hard work Rosemary and Beth did for me. This play would not be what it is without their assistance.

Directing *Willpower* has been an amazing experience. I looked forward to every rehearsal, researching each character, and also learning more about the community in which I live. *Willpower* is a production that everyone can relate to, whether you are a history buff or a theatre and music enthusiast. It is a play that warms hearts and tickles the mind.

The Story Behind *Willpower*

by Playwright Tyler Tichelaar

Playwright Tyler R. Tichelaar

In August, 2013, when Kaye Hiebel and Jessica "Red" Bays asked me to write a play as a fundraiser for the Marquette Regional History Center, I was hesitant, considering myself a novelist, not a playwright. But when they shared with me their vision of bringing Will Adams' story to the stage, I instantly saw its dramatic possibilities and how it would speak to modern audiences as a true tale of overcoming adversity.

I already knew the basics of Will Adams' story. He was born in 1878 and adopted as a young child by prominent Marquette businessman Sidney Adams and his wife Harriet. Will was a talented singer in the boys choir at St. Paul's Episcopal Church, played baseball, and by the time he was a teenager, was considered a literary expert by Marquette residents.

But in his late boyhood, Will developed a life-changing disability. The tissues in his legs began to harden until they became immoveable—a disease the Victorians termed ossification. Numerous doctors were consulted, but none could explain the disease's cause.

For most active boys, the diagnosis would have been earth-shattering. But Will took it as a challenge to accomplish all he could before the ossification took over his entire body. For as long as possible, he employed his hands, drawing countless cartoons of notable locals such as Nathan Kaufman and Peter White. He wrote poetry and essays and began the magazine *CHIPS*, illustrating it himself. Unable to sell magazine ads in person, he did it over the telephone, eventually having an attendant hold the receiver for him.

One of Will's frequent visitors was his good friend Norma Ross, a music teacher in the Marquette Public Schools. In 1905, Will and Norma wrote an operetta titled *Miss D.Q. Pons*. Will composed the music in his head and hummed the tunes for Norma, who wrote down the notes. Later, Norma starred in the production, which toured the Upper Peninsula. Will attended the performances, traveling by railroad in a portable bed.

When I agreed to write the play, I felt I already knew quite a lot about Will, but I wanted to know more about Norma Ross before I began. With the help of Marquette Regional History Center research librarians Rosemary Michelin and Beth Gruber, I learned Norma's father had owned one of the first theatres in Marquette, Mather Hall, so at an early age, Norma was exposed to music and the theatre, and she developed her musical gift by singing in the First Baptist Church's choir. Frank B. Spear, Sr. of Marquette offered to finance sending her to New York to be in the theatre there, but her father opposed his daughter having a "life upon the wicked stage." Instead, she went to Northwestern University to become a music teacher. She returned to Marquette to teach in the public schools and also be very active in community theatre and music productions for decades.

In *Willpower*, I wanted to bring Will and Norma and their family members and friends to life. Artistic license was taken to fill in some gaps in their stories, but I tried my best to represent them truthfully.

Besides Will and Norma, I knew Will's family had to play a major role in the play. After all, if Will had not been adopted by the wealthy Adams family, imagine what his life would have been like dealing with his ossification. Fortunately, Will's loving adoptive parents had the money to care for him as well as possible. His parents called in the best doctors to try to help him, and he did have a portable bed so he could go to church and later travel by railroad when *Miss D.Q. Pons* toured the Upper Michigan.

I had already known that Bertha Adams outlived her parents and Will and was the last to live in the Adams house, but I knew nothing of her private life. Now, in researching the family, I discovered that she had been married twice. She married her first husband, George Beard, on December 20, 1888 in a private wedding in the Adams home, as reported in the *Mining Journal*. They were married less than seventeen months when tragedy struck.

I never learned the cause of George's death, but ironically, the Marquette *Mining Journal* on May 9, 1890 stated that Mr. Adams was leaving for Tyler, Texas because of his son-in-law's death there; ironically, by chance, I happened to spot in the same issue the announcement that Dr. Dawson had just moved to Marquette and opened offices. That coincidence felt like fate to me—a sure sign that Bertha and Dr. Dawson's love was meant to be. Of course, how they met and fell in love, I don't know, but it seemed logical that if he were a doctor, he would have been called in to attend to Will. What better way to weave a romance between them and show how significant Will was in their lives. And while no poem appeared in *CHIPS* from the doctor, Will obviously loved to be witty and he was very fond of his brother-in-law as evidenced by other mentions of the doctor in *CHIPS* as well as cartoons Will drew of him.

I'm sure most people who see or read *Willpower* wonder what the truth is about Will and Norma's own relationship. We don't know for certain whether they were in love, but we do know that Norma never married, despite the *Mining Journal* naming her the most popular girl in Marquette in her youth. We know that Norma did visit Will constantly, she did write the music for *Miss D.Q. Pons*, and Will did specifically create the title role for her. We also know that Norma was out of town visiting Grace and some friends in Detroit and in Ohio when Will died because the *Mining Journal* reported that she returned to town on Thursday night, August 12, 1909, the night before Will's funeral. Obviously, she rushed home for his funeral, although no telegram remains that she was notified of his death.

Will's own death was actually a surprise to everyone. The *Mining Journal* reported on Wednesday, August 11, 1909, that friends were "shocked" by his sudden demise. His actual cause of death was said to be heart failure after a sudden attack of intestinal poisoning. His mother and an attending physician and nurses were at his bedside and he was conscious to the end.

We also know that Lillian Russell did visit Will, and most likely, Norma was present. The visit occurred around the time Russell appeared in *Wildfire* at the Marquette Opera House on Saturday, June 5, 1909, for which she received great applause and reviews in the *Daily Marquette Mining Journal*. She recalled her visit to Will later in an article she wrote titled "A Tribute to Genius" as follows:

Will's cartoon of Dr. Dawson

> The physical body often becomes paralyzed and leaves only the mind to live, sometimes, for years. I knew a remarkable case of a brilliant man who lived at Marquette, Michigan, who was a perfect illustration of this theory. He was helpless in body, blind also, and yet he was a poet and edited a newspaper.

> He wrote the libretto of a comic opera which was produced. He was wheeled into the theatre to hear plays. When I called upon him, in his own rooms, he entertained me so charmingly by singing his own opera over to me that I never thought for a moment of his afflictions, but thoroughly enjoyed his humor and wonderful brain.

Two weeks before *Willpower* premiered, the Marquette Regional History Center found in its archives an autographed photo from Russell. The wording on it isn't perfectly clear, but it seems to say, "To Will Adams, with My Sympathy, of Lillian Russell." Perhaps she gave the photo to Will when they met, or more likely, she heard of his death and sent it to his family. The photo was later given as a gift by Norma Ross to the Marquette History Museum, so either the family gave it to her or she received it from Lillian Russell directly; either way, that the photo was in Norma's possession is a clear sign of Will and Norma's close relationship. The cast and I interpreted the discovery of this photo as a sure sign that Norma and Will knew what we were about and were watching over us, glad to be remembered and hinting that we were on the right track in telling their story.

Despite the poetic license taken to tie together the play's plot elements, I worked in as many of Will's actual words and expressions into the play as possible, as well as historical facts. For example, Will was visited not long before his death by a reporter from the *Detroit Free Press*. During the interview, he told the reporter, "Don't call me a cripple when you write your story, and don't say I am bedridden. I don't like those expressions. They put a fellow off, you know.... Had it been otherwise, I might have become the subject of a trust investigation committee or a bank president. And I'd rather be literary than sordid any day." While there wasn't room in the play for a scene with the reporter, I inserted these words into one of Will's comments to Lillian Russell when she suggests someone write a book about him.

In another scene, Will tells Norma he will be her Svengali, a reference to the villain in George du Maurier's 1894 novel *Trilby*. The novel, which in some ways is like an earlier version of *The Phantom of the Opera*, was immensely popular in its time, and I knew Will was familiar with it because one of his cartoons is of what appears to be a gorilla reading the novel. It only felt fitting then that in his relationship with Norma, Will would think of himself as a type of Svengali to his singer friend. Many of Will's writings were also used throughout the play, including his poem "Summertime in Marquette," and the speech he makes as the Wooden Man, which I borrowed from his book *Old Saws with New Teeth* and only slightly altered to work as a dramatic monologue.

Music was so important to Will and Norma that I knew it had to be an integral part of the production. While no copy of *Miss D.Q. Pons* could be found, the playbill and the advertisements and reviews all helped me to recreate a scene from the operetta to give the audience a taste of what it might have been like. The playbill was quite elaborate and listed the titles of all the songs, the cast, and also a summary of the plot. The play was based on an American heiress marrying an English Lord, and besides Miss D.Q. Pons, the characters of Lord Breakus and Colonel Foster were in the play. The play had a song titled "When the Moon Is Softly Beaming," for which I substituted "Mr. Moon-Man, Turn Off the Light" which would have been in spirit with the lost song. This song is attributed to Jack Noworth and was written as a sequel to "Shine on, Harvest Moon." It was first sung in the 1911 show *Little Miss Fix-It* and is an example of the type of music Will and Norma might have written for the show.

The other period songs used in *Willpower* include, "After the Ball," which originally appeared in the

Broadway musical *A Trip to Chinatown* in 1891. It was the first song ever to sell over one million copies of sheet music, and we know from an article written by Norma's sister Grace, in which she recalled musical events at their father's theatre, Mather Hall, that it was sung there. The hymn "How Can I Keep from Singing" was inserted to reflect Will's years singing in the boys choir at St. Paul's and because it was the most vibrant hymn of the period I could find that reflected his positive spirit. Finally, that Will would write a love song for Norma was director Moire Embley's idea. The result was "You Will Not Love Me," composed by Jeff Bruning, whose knowledge of the period's music made it fit right in with the other music, and hopefully, my tongue-in-cheek lyrics were in keeping with Will's sense of humor. Additional period background music was selected and played by Jeff throughout the performance.

Will's Cartoon of a Gorilla Reading *Trilby*

Because of the timeframe of the play, few people alive today remembered Norma Ross, who died at age ninety in January, 1973. However, Fred Rydholm had passed away only in 2009 and had been well-loved by the community. He really had appeared in *Brigadoon* and presented Norma with an award that night in 1963. I made sure I got the blessing of the Rydholm family to depict him in the play. Then, only a couple of weeks before the play premiered, the museum found the *Brigadoon* program from that production and I discovered that Vivian Lasich, my eighth grade English teacher, had been the director of the play. Mrs. Lasich happened to be in the audience the night *Willpower* premiered, so Jessica made a point of naming her when, as Norma, she referred to the play's director. Fred Rydholm's son, Dan, was also in the audience, and he had told me as a young boy he remembered his father dressed as Mr. Lundy from *Brigadoon* that night. Also present was my great-aunt, Sadie White Johnson Merchant, who had known Norma Ross and had earlier informed me that Norma and her mother, my great-grandmother, had been good friends and both members of the First Baptist Church. The past and the present would feel linked that night, as if Will and Norma and the world they knew had existed only yesterday, and they were still a vital part of Marquette's community.

But there was a long journey between writing the play and bringing it to the stage. I shared my various drafts of *Willpower* with Moire Embley, Jessica "Red" Bays, and other members of the Marquette Regional History Center staff, and a few close friends, all of whom offered feedback and suggestions. In the process, I learned not only to consider plot and character development, but how to work in set and costume changes between scenes, and what was possible within our budget limitations. Fortunately, our budget, initially provided by the Marquette Regional History Center, was enhanced through a generous grant from the Michigan Humanities Council and matching grants from the Marquette Community Foundation and Upper Peninsula Health Plan.

While rehearsals began, the Marquette Regional History Center did a fabulous job promoting the play for months beforehand, especially through giving previews of it in many of their historical presentations throughout the summer. Andy Vanwelsenaers, who played the older Will, was in costume as part of the historic cemetery tours that summer to tell Will's story at his gravesite in Park Cemetery as well as on the historic bus tours. The bus tours are designed to take a group of history enthusiasts on a bus ride through Marquette and stop at various historical locations where a person dressed as a historical figure boards the bus to tell his or her story at a location associated with that person. Jessica "Red" Bays got the daytime Emmy for her performance as Norma Ross on the bus tours one afternoon when an unexpected event happened. She arrived outside the Adams House shortly before the bus came. Dressed as a 1960s Norma Ross, complete with silver-gray wig and polyester pants suit, she waited outside the Adams House, now the Terrace Apartments, pacing up and down in front of the house and repeating her lines to herself to be prepared when the bus arrived. Her performance was so convincing that a concerned neighbor chose to call the police to report a strange woman outside. The officer showed up, parked his patrol car, got out of the car, and approached Jessica with a piece of paper he began to hand to her just as the bus pulled up. A true actor, Jessica did not want to step out of character and spoil her performance for the audience on the bus, so she ignored the officer and began waving to the bus. The bus stopped and she jumped onboard, gave a great performance, was applauded, and then left the bus. The police officer then left as well, realizing she wasn't a crazy woman.

Meanwhile, rehearsals had begun. Because of the Lake Superior Youth Theatre's involvement, several young actors were cast, and that required some late changes to the script, including changing the ages of Norma and Will to fit the actors cast. While the play had been written with Will as fifteen in the early scenes, his age was changed to eleven for the performance and Norma's role was also made younger; consequently, some of the years of the scenes also had to be slightly altered. However, in keeping with historical accuracy, I have left the original ages and dates for Will and Norma in the published script.

Many minor rewrites were made throughout the rehearsal process, from cutting lines that were too long to memorize or rewording sentences that came off awkwardly when spoken. I was, however, stunned by the magic that actors brought to the written word, and Moire's direction impressed me as I saw her coach the actors on how to say their lines or how to move about in ways different from what I initially envisioned, but which all enhanced the production. I was also pleased by all of the coverage we received from the local radio, newspaper, and television media during the rehearsals, including the television stations coming to film clips from the dress rehearsal for the evening news, which definitely helped the ticket sales.

Jessica "Red" Bays as Norma Ross on the steps of the Adams House during the history bus tours

The night before opening was the tech rehearsal, and that was the first night the cast could actually rehearse on the stage in Kaufman Auditorium where the performance would be held. Prior to that, rehearsals had been done, fittingly, in the Fred Rydholm atrium at the History Center. The night of the tech rehearsal, I became very nervous. I had never attended a tech rehearsal before, and throughout all the rehearsals, I never got a clear idea of how long the play would be because only certain scenes were rehearsed at a time. The night of the tech rehearsal took five hours as technical issues were resolved and everyone became comfortable with the setting, but by the end of the night, I was terrified everything would go wrong, and it would be a colossal flop. Nevertheless, everyone assured me this night was typical of tech rehearsals.

Opening night, I was smiling while trying to hide how nervous I truly was as I greeted everyone who had come to see the performance. And then the curtain went up and the audience started to laugh at all the jokes in the play, which sounded so much better than I had written them when delivered by the talented actors. I can't even begin to say what it feels like to hear hundreds of people laugh at a joke you wrote and confirm it is funny.

There were a few bloopers that night. In the first act, Will's drawings weren't placed on the table beside him, but Allison Hyttinen, playing Bertha, did a fabulous job of ad libbing her lines and then sneaking in the drawings later with the tea tray. No one in the audience noticed the omission. The audience did notice, however, a loud bang that happened when a leg on the couch broke off and rolled across the stage and into the orchestra pit. No one knew what had caused the noise, though, and remarkably, the couch stayed in position with only three legs.

During intermission, people began to congratulate me and I overheard people saying how much they enjoyed it. Even better, during the second act, I could hear what sounded like rows of people behind me crying. Somehow, I had pulled off writing a play that touched people, though I never could have done it without the support of the Marquette Regional History Center staff and their vision for the play, or the exhausting work of director Moire Embley, or the dedication and talent of a wonderful cast and crew.

I was relieved when the final curtain came down, but I was also so proud of everyone involved. Truly, there aren't too many things more thrilling for a playwright than to experience his words translated onto the stage.

I hope *Willpower* continues to speak to everyone who hears its story. It is a testament to what can be accomplished against all odds. It is a tale of the human spirit enduring and succeeding. I hope from now on that you will think, like I do, that "If Will Adams could do what he did while confined to a bed and unable to move, there's no reason why I can't accomplish anything I put my mind to."

Ernie Ludlow's Crazy Pants

Ernie Ludlow was a real person who did tour with an acting company before appearing in *Miss D.Q. Pons*, being billed as T.E. Ludlow. While I have made him appear as a bit of a rival to Will, and it is true he was replaced by Clarence Brown in later productions of the play, he was obviously good friends with Will as made clear in the poem itself that Will wrote about his pants.

The poem appeared in the July 23, 1898 issue of *CHIPS* as follows:

TO MY OWNLIEST ONE

———

The Following lines were inspired by a pair of English riding trowsers which made their initial appearance in Marquette Sunday last.

The verses are respectfully dedicated to my warm friend Ernest Ludlow, of Negaunee:

———

LUDDY'S ENGLISH PANTS

I've seen a heap of things in life
Since I've been born, my friends,
Unusual things and common things,
And little odds and ends.
I've seen them in the day time
And I've seen them late at night;
I've seen them when quite sober
And I've seen 'em pretty tight.
I've traveled from Chicago to the gulf of Mexico
An I'm just a writing this thing
For to let the people know
That in all my various travels
With my Uncles and my Aunts
I've never seen a dog-gone thing
Like Luddy's English Pants.

I've seen the dusky Spaniard
With pants a heap too small
And I've seen the little greaser kids with no pants on at all.
In Frisco too, I've seen the Chinamen in snowy trouserets
That looked for all the world like mine when I wore pantalets;
Then too, I've seen the bloomer kind made of mosquito bar,
Heaven, I shall call a halt before I go too far.
And simply say that all these styles
Were only to enhance the beauty of and emphasize
Those nobby English Pants.

I've dreamed of pants, and worn pants too,
When just a little kid.
And come to think about it now
Ma made my first, she did,
Then sent me off to Sunday school
One glorious Easter day
The happiest kid in all the world,
My pants had come to stay.
But then I never knew some day
I should have cause to pine,
Because another fellow's pants
Were better ones than mine.
But ah! alas, I know it now,
I saw it at a glance
On Sunday last, when I beheld
Friend Luddy's English Pants.

Now, when from life's uncertain coil
I have to shuffle off
You'll [not] find me in the sky
A learning to play golf.
Nor wasting time a hanging round
The golden gates to see
If any of my friends got in
As easy as me.
Oh no! far greater things than these
Shall occupy my mind,
And if you just observe me close
Undoubtedly you'll find
me using all my eloquence
Whe 'ere I get a chance
To plead for the fac simile of Luddy's English Pants.

WILL S. ADAMS

I daresay Ernie's pants weren't all that bad. After all, they were English pants; perhaps they helped to persuade Will to cast him as the English Lord Breakus a few years later.

Marquette Regional History Center
Presents....

Poster Image
Designed by Corey Sustarich

Tickets available at NMU EZ Ticket Outlet
starting August 1st
www.nmu.edu/tickets or 906.227.1032
$15.00 in advance
$20.00 at the door

Willpower

An Original Play Written by Tyler Tichelaar
Directed by Moire Embley
Musical Direction by Jeff Bruning
September 18 & 19, 7:00 p.m.
at Kaufman Auditorium

Will Adams a Marquette boy, his name is synonymous with the sheer will it took for him to survive his late boyhood years to the age of 32. In early adolescence his soft tissues were becoming hard, gradually turning him into a living statue. It was the late 1800's and physicians of the day were baffled. Others faced with such a dark future might have felt sorry for themselves and turned inward. Not so for Will. His disease brought about a creative burst of energy. This is a story not only about one young man's perseverance, but about the Marquette community members who came together in support of his creative endeavors. Join us for this amazing story of love, wit, mind over matter, and the relationships that Will fostered within his short life!

 For more information please visit marquettehistory.org,
like our event on Facebook or call (906) 226-3571.

Michigan **Humanities** Council

**Upper Peninsula
Health Plan**

Marquette County
community foundation

Music from *Willpower*

After the Ball
interpolated into A TRIP TO CHINATOWN

Arr. by JOS. CLAUDER.

Words amd Music by
CHARLES K. HARRIS

Tempo di Valse,

1. A lit‑tle maid‑‑en climbed an old man's knee............
2. Bright lights were flash‑‑ing in the grand ball‑room,............
3. Long years have passed child,......... I've nev‑er wed,............

Begged for a sto‑ry— "Do Un‑cle please.".........
Soft ly the mu‑sic, play‑ing sweet tunes............
True to my lost love, though she is dead..........

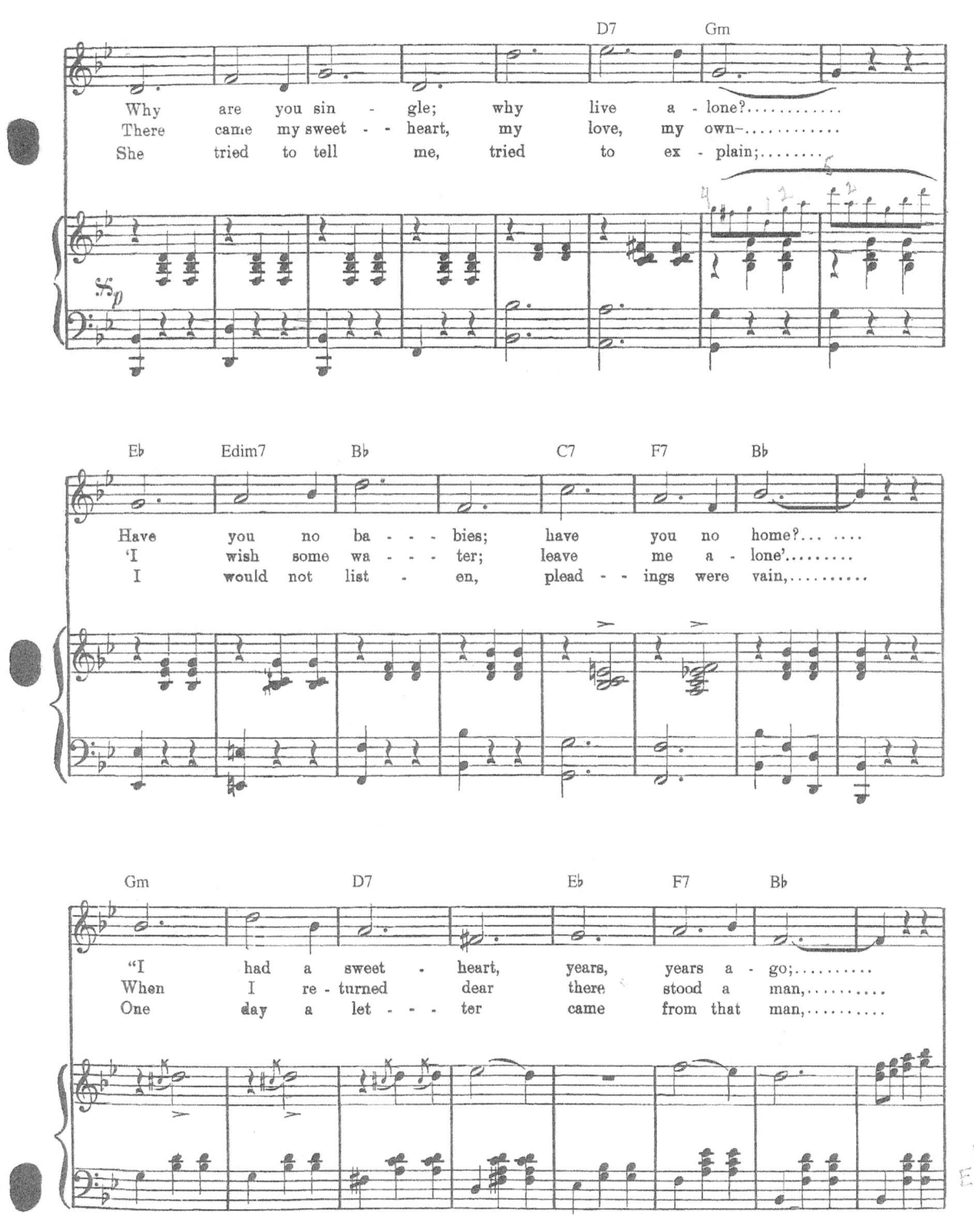

How Can I Keep from Singing

² Mister Moon-Man Turn Off The Light.

By Nora Bayes and
Jack Norworth.

When the moon is shin - ing yel - low, _____
All you lads and lit - tle miss - es, _____

And a girl - ie with her fel - low, _____
Like to have your hugs and kiss - es, _____

Both are get - ting nice and mel - low, In the
But re - mem - ber half the bliss is, When it's

bright moon - light. _____
dark as it can be. _____

Then the light-man will dis - cov - er, _____
If once more I start my plead - ing, _____

Sweet-hearts keep-ing un - der cov - er, _____
Tell him dark-ness we are need - ing, _____ In

Soon he hears that girl and lov - er, Say to
case my plead - ing he is heed - ing, You must

Mister Moon-Man etc. 4

I'll take my la - dy to a shad - y place where I can

hug my ba - by, And we'll say to you, "Good - night," "Good - night!" We

want to tease and squeeze, if you please, Mis - ter Moon-Man

turn off the light.   light.

Mister Moon-Man etc. 4

You Will Not Love Me

Music by Jeff Bruning
Words by Tyler Tichelaar

Photos from the Original Production

Act 1 Scene 1

Act 1 Scene 2

Act 1 Scene 3

Act 1 Scene 4

Act 1 Scene 5

Act 1 Scene 5

Act 1 Scene 6

Act 1 Scene 7

Act 1 Scene 8

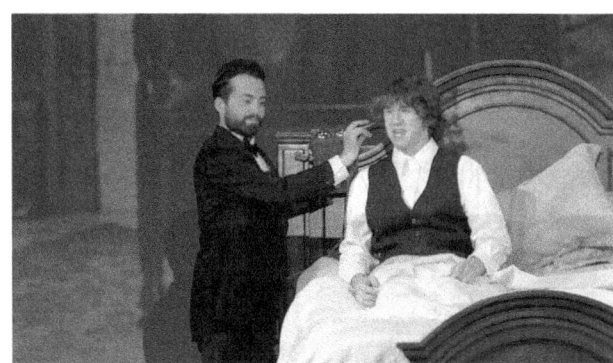

Act 1 Scene 9

Act 1 Scene 10

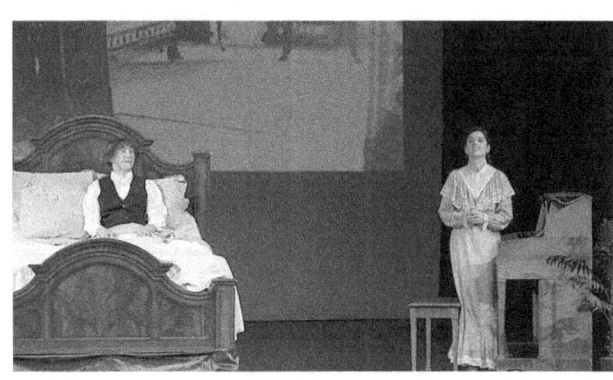

Act 1 Scene 11

Act 2 Scene 1

Act 2 Scene 2

Act 2 Scene 2

Act 2 Scene 2

Act 2 Scene 3

Act 2 Scene 4

Act 2 Scene 5

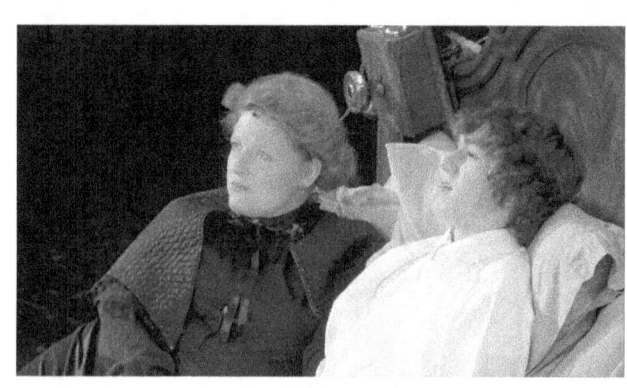

Act 2 Scene 6

Act 2 Scene 6

Act 2 Scene 7

Act 2 Scene 8

Act 2 Scene 9

Curtain Call

A video of the original *Willpower* production is available from the
Marquette Regional History Center.
www.MarquetteHistory.org

About the Author

Tyler R. Tichelaar is a seventh generation resident of Marquette, Michigan. Since age eight he wanted to be a writer, and at age sixteen, he began writing his first novel, which years later was published as *The Only Thing That Lasts*.

Tyler has a Ph.D. in Literature from Western Michigan University, and Bachelor and Master's Degrees in English from Northern Michigan University. He is the current President of the Upper Peninsula Publishers and Authors Association. He is the owner of Marquette Fiction and Superior Book Productions, a professional book review, editing, and proofreading service.

In 2009, Tyler was awarded the Best Historical Fiction Award in the Reader Views Literary Awards for his novel *Narrow Lives*. He has since gone on to sponsor that award. In 2011, he received the Barb H. Kelly Historic Preservation Award from the Marquette Beautification and Restoration Committee for his book *My Marquette* and he received the Marquette County Arts Award that same year for an "Outstanding Writer."

Today, Tyler continues to live in Marquette, where the roar of Lake Superior, mountains of snow, and sandstone architecture inspire his writing. He has many future books in the planning.

Be Sure to Read All of Tyler R. Tichelaar's Marquette Books

IRON PIONEERS:
THE MARQUETTE TRILOGY: BOOK ONE

When iron ore is discovered in Michigan's Upper Peninsula in the 1840s, newlyweds Gerald Henning and his beautiful socialite wife Clara travel from Boston to the little village of Marquette on the shores of Lake Superior. They and their companions, Irish and German immigrants, French Canadians, and fellow New Englanders face blizzards and near starvation, devastating fires, and financial hardships. Yet these iron pioneers persevere until their wilderness village becomes integral to the Union cause in the Civil War and then a prosperous modern city. Meticulously researched, warmly written, and spanning half a century, *Iron Pioneers* is a testament to the spirit that forged America.

THE QUEEN CITY
THE MARQUETTE TRILOGY: BOOK TWO

During the first half of the twentieth century, Marquette grows into the Queen City of the North. Here is the tale of a small town undergoing change as its horses are replaced by streetcars and automobiles, and its pioneers are replaced by new generations who prosper despite two World Wars and the Great Depression. Margaret Dalrymple finds her Scottish prince, though he is neither Scottish nor a prince. Molly Bergmann becomes an inspiration to her grandchildren. Jacob Whitman's children engage in a family feud. The Queen City's residents marry, divorce, have children, die, break their hearts, go to war, gossip, blackmail, raise families, move away, and then return to Marquette. And always, always they are in love with the haunting land that is their home.

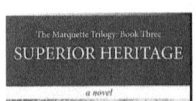

SUPERIOR HERITAGE
THE MARQUETTE TRILOGY: BOOK THREE

The Marquette Trilogy comes to a satisfying conclusion as it brings together characters and plots from the earlier novels and culminates with Marquette's sesquicentennial celebrations in 1999. What happened to Madeleine Henning is finally revealed as secrets from the past shed light upon the present. Marquette's residents struggle with a difficult local economy, yet remain optimistic for the future. The novel's main character, John Vandelaare, is descended from all the early Marquette families in *Iron Pioneers* and *The Queen City*. While he cherishes his family's past, he questions whether he should remain in his hometown. Then an event happens that will change his life forever.

NARROW LIVES

Narrow Lives is the story of those whose lives were affected by Lysander Blackmore, the sinister banker first introduced to readers in *The Queen City*. It is a novel that stands alone, yet readers of *The Marquette Trilogy* will be reacquainted with some familiar characters. Written as a collection of connected short stories, each told in first person by a different character, *Narrow Lives* depicts the influence one person has, even in death, upon others, and it explores the prisons of grief, loneliness, and fear self-created when people doubt their own worthiness.

THE ONLY THING THAT LASTS

The story of Robert O'Neill, the famous novelist introduced in *The Marquette Trilogy*. As a young boy during World War I, Robert is forced to leave his South Carolina home to live in Marquette with his grandmother and aunt. He finds there a cold climate, but many warmhearted friends. An old-fashioned story that follows Robert's growth from childhood to successful writer and husband, the novel is written as Robert O'Neill's autobiography, his final gift to Marquette by memorializing the town of his youth.

SPIRIT OF THE NORTH: A PARANORMAL ROMANCE

In 1873, orphaned sisters Barbara and Adele Traugott travel to Upper Michigan to live with their uncle, only to find he is deceased. Penniless, they are forced to spend the long, fierce winter alone in their uncle's remote wilderness cabin. Frightened yet determined, the sisters face blizzards and near starvation to survive. Amid their difficulties, they find love and heartache—and then, a ghostly encounter and the coming of spring lead them to discovering the true miracle of their being.

THE BEST PLACE

An irritating best friend gained during a childhood spent in a Catholic orphanage, a father who became a Communist and went to Russia in the 1930s, and 3:00 a.m. visits to The Pancake House. Such is the life of Lyla Hopewell. But in the summer of 2005, when her old boyfriend Bill has a heart attack, her best friend Bel really gets on her nerves, and Finn Fest comes to Marquette, things will change for Lyla.

Joined by a cast of Marquette's most eccentric and endearing characters—the foul-mouthed fourteen-year-old Josie; ninety-three-year-old Eleanor, still trying to fix her little brother's love life; ex-boyfriend and blunt womanizer, Bill; blind Mary Mitchell and her ornery sister Florence; the sweet but romantically confused cabdriver Sybil; and many, many more—Lyla recounts her life-story as she comes to terms with her past. After years of feeling unloved, neglected, frustrated, and unfulfilled, can Lyla finally find her own best place?

For more information on Tyler's Marquette Books, visit:

www.MarquetteFiction.com

Be sure also to check out Tyler's nonfiction titles

MY MARQUETTE:
EXPLORE THE QUEEN CITY OF THE NORTH
—ITS HISTORY, PEOPLE, AND PLACES

My Marquette is the result of its author's lifelong love affair with his hometown. Join Tyler R. Tichelaar, seventh generation Marquette resident and author of *The Marquette Trilogy*, as he takes you on a tour of the history, people, and places of Marquette. Stories of the past and present, both true and fictional, will leave you understanding why Marquette really is "The Queen City of the North." Along the way, Tyler will describe his own experiences growing up in Marquette, recall family and friends he knew, and give away secrets about the people behind the characters in his novels. *My Marquette* offers a rare insight into an author's creation of fiction and a refreshing view of a city's history and relevance to today. Reading *My Marquette* is equal to being given a personal tour by someone who knows Marquette intimately.

KING ARTHUR'S CHILDREN:
A STUDY IN FICTION AND TRADITION

The first full-length analysis of every known treatment of King Arthur's children, from Welsh legends and French romances, to Scottish genealogies and modern novels by such authors as Parke Godwin, Stephen Lawhead, Debra Kemp, and Elizabeth Wein. *King Arthur's Children* explores an often overlooked theme in Arthurian literature and reveals King Arthur's bloodline may still exist today.

THE GOTHIC WANDERER:
FROM TRANSGRESSION TO REDEMPTION

Tichelaar examines the figure of the Gothic wanderer in such well-known Gothic novels as *The Mysteries of Udolpho*, *Frankenstein*, and *Dracula*, as well as lesser known works like Fanny Burney's *The Wanderer*, Mary Shelley's *The Last Man*, and Edward Bulwer-Lytton's *Zanoni*. He also finds surprising Gothic elements in classics like Dickens' *A Tale of Two Cities* and Edgar Rice Burroughs' *Tarzan of the Apes*. From Matthew Lewis' *The Monk* to Stephenie Meyer's *Twilight*, Tichelaar explores a literary tradition whose characters reflect our greatest fears and deepest hopes. Readers will find here the revelation that not only are we all Gothic wanderers—but we are so only by our own choosing.

CREATING A LOCAL HISTORICAL BOOK:
FICTION AND NONFICTION GENRES

In this short book, Tyler Tichelaar, author of *My Marquette* and The Marquette Trilogy, talks in an interview format about how he became interested in writing both local history and regional and historical fiction and his research and writing process to bring his books to fruition.

And Tyler's new series

THE CHILDREN OF ARTHUR

ARTHUR'S LEGACY:
THE CHILDREN OF ARTHUR, BOOK ONE

All his life, Adam Morgan has sought his true identity and the father he never knew. When multiple coincidences lead him to England, he will not only find his father, but mutual love with a woman he can never have, and a family legacy he never imagined possible. Among England's green hills and crumbling castles, Adam's intuition awakens, and when a mysterious stranger appears with a tale of Britain's past, Adam discovers forces may be at work to bring about the return of a king.

MELUSINE'S GIFT:
THE CHILDREN OF ARTHUR, BOOK TWO

Following his father's death, Adam Delaney has acquired his father's title as Earl of Delaney and married Anne, who has given birth to their twin sons, Lance and Tristan. Now Adam and Anne have taken a much-needed vacation in France, leaving their sons at Delaney Castle with Adam's mother and grandmother and Anne's father.

But what begins as a pleasant and long overdue honeymoon soon becomes another strange mythical adventure when Anne reunites with her old friend, Morgan, while the couple is visiting Lusignan, home to the legendary fairy Melusine. Before Anne knows it, she finds herself listening to stories within stories about the fairy Melusine and the magical rings she left to her children, magical rings that are tied to Adam and Anne's future in ways they can scarcely imagine.

and Coming Soon:

OGIER'S PRAYER: THE CHILDREN OF ARTHUR, BOOK THREE

LILITH'S LOVE: THE CHILDREN OF ARTHUR, BOOK FOUR

ARTHUR'S BOSOM: THE CHILDREN OF ARTHUR, BOOK FIVE

For updates on Tyler R. Tichelaar's Arthurian novels, visit:

www.ChildrenofArthur.com

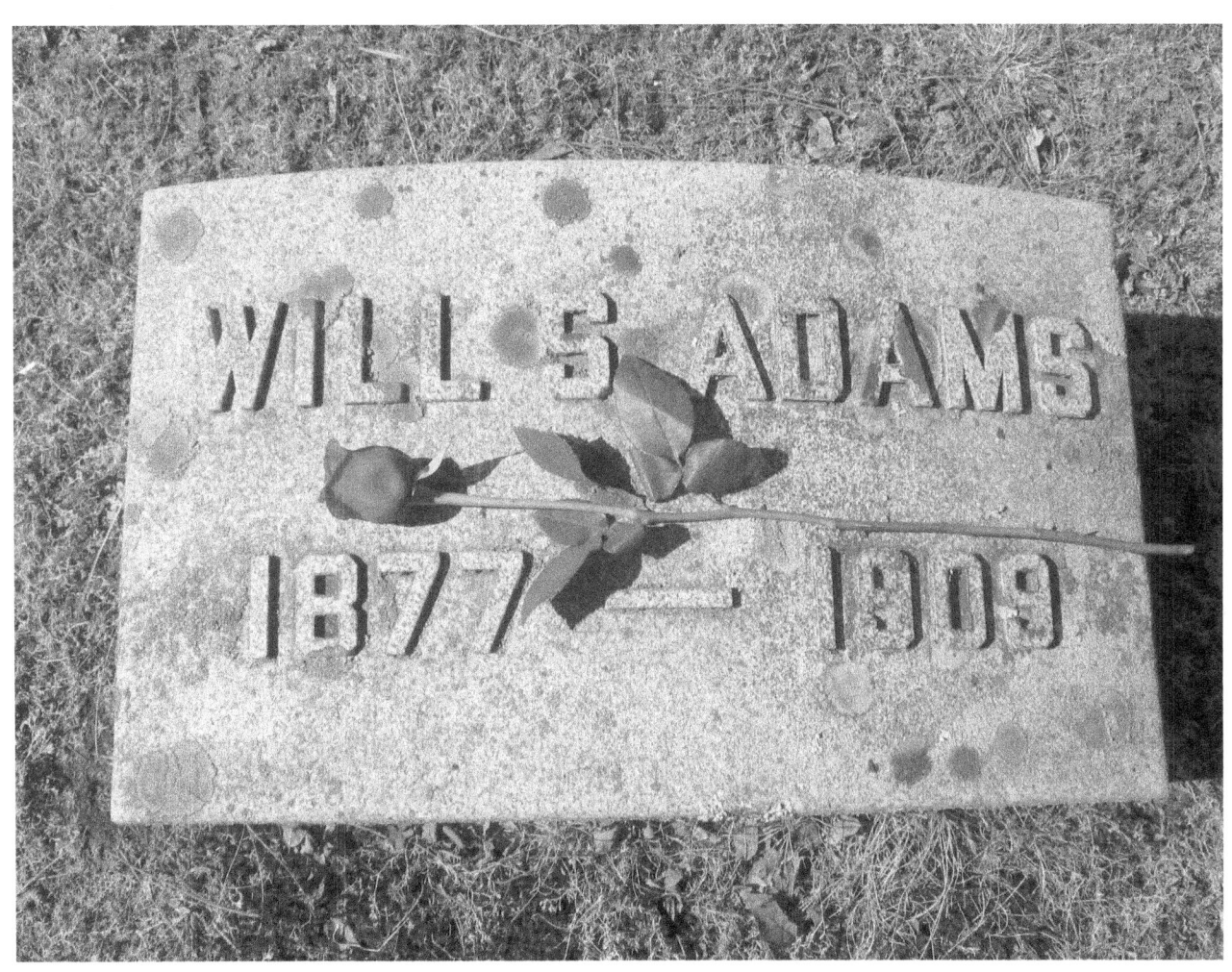